CYPRUS DREAM

Lorna had come to Cyprus reluctantly, as her aunt's holiday companion. There she met James, who helped her to find out that there was more to the island than hotels and beaches. But could he save her when a ruthless scheme to exploit the island's beauty put her in deadly danger? What would happen to their growing friendship when the holiday was over? And what were her aunt's secret plans?

SHEILA HOLROYD

CYPRUS DREAM

Complete and Unabridged

LINFORD
Leicester

First published in Great Britain in 2009

First Linford Edition
published 2010

British Library CIP Data

Holroyd, Sheila.
    Cyprus dream. - - (Linford romance library)
    1. Cyprus- -Fiction. 2. Romantic suspense
novels. 3. Large type books.
    I. Title II. Series
    823.9'2–dc22

    ISBN 978–1–44480–376–1

Published by
F. A. Thorpe (Publishing)
Anstey, Leicestershire

Set by Words & Graphics Ltd.
Anstey, Leicestershire
Printed and bound in Great Britain by
T. J. International Ltd., Padstow, Cornwall

This book is printed on acid-free paper

1

Aunt Anne's voice pierced the crowd around the luggage carousel. 'There's my case coming now, Lorna! Make sure you catch it!'

Lorna, who had already seen the case coming and had positioned herself to grab it, gritted her teeth, seized the handle of the suitcase and swung it off the carousel.

'Ouch!' a voice protested. The case had hit a young man on his shins.

'Sorry,' Lorna said briefly.

'You didn't see me. It wasn't your fault. Now, if you could just move a little . . . I can see my case coming . . . '

He moved forward, stumbling on the case Lorna had rescued, and almost fell. By the time he had recovered his balance, his case had sailed by and he was left looking after it helplessly.

Soon Lorna had spotted and seized

her own case and made her way to where Aunt Anne was waiting with a trolley. Eager to escape from the airport, Lorna loaded the cases on the trolley and pushed. Apparently stuck, the trolley did not move. She pushed again impatiently — hard — and the trolley shot forward, straight into the legs of the young man whom Lorna had already injured.

'Sorry,' Lorna muttered again as she and her aunt made for the exit where the travel rep was waiting for them.

'Miss Short and Miss Evans for the Hotel Persepolis? Coach nine, on the left over there.'

Gratefully Lorna saw the driver stow the cases in the hold of the coach as they took their seats inside.

'We are just waiting for one more passenger,' the rep told them. 'Apparently he has had trouble with his luggage. Ah, here he is now.'

It was the young man, visibly limping, who surrendered his luggage to the driver and climbed aboard. The coach set off abruptly and the travel rep welcomed the passengers to Cyprus and began to tell them about Paphos.

'It's a wonderful place. There is something for everyone — beaches, restaurants, archaeological sites. You are going to enjoy yourselves.'

Aunt Anne, who had been to Paphos several times already, ignored the rep and gazed out at the scenery lit by the September sunshine, pointing out landmarks she remembered to Lorna. After a while she began to frown.

'There are a lot more houses than I remember,' she said uncertainly. 'And some of them are ruining the beautiful hillsides.'

'Well, Cyprus is a popular place to live, and people need houses,' Lorna remarked, only half-listening.

The resort of Paphos was not far from the airport and soon holidaymakers were being dropped off at their hotels.

'This is the Persepolis,' Aunt Anne said, already gathering up her coat and handbag. Lorna followed her off the coach and stood for a moment gazing up at the hotel's impressive exterior.

'Come along, Lorna. We've got to register,' Aunt Anne urged impatiently.

'Coming,' Lorna said, still looking up as she stepped backwards.

'Ow!' There came a yelp from behind her.

She had stepped back on the foot of the young man.

'Sorry,' she said automatically.

He glared at her wordlessly and she noticed how he pointedly avoided coming anywhere near her as the receptionist, whose badge identified her as Katerina, rapidly and competently took their details and gave them their room keys.

Aunt Anne had insisted, to Lorna's relief, that they should have separate rooms. They reached the third floor and her aunt opened the door of her room, walked straight through it, and opened the glass doors leading to the balcony.

'There!' she said dramatically.

The view was marvellous. Lorna

looked out across the hotel's palm-filled gardens, across the blue sea, to a narrow spit of land.

'That's Paphos harbour,' her aunt indicated. 'It's a wonderful place to sit and have a coffee and watch the world go by. We'll go there tomorrow. Now, I need a shower, so I'll see you later.'

Dismissed, Lorna crossed the corridor to her own room. Unlike her aunt's room, this looked out on to a busy road. Well, that might provide some interesting spectacles, Lorna mused. She sank down on the large, soft bed, laid back and closed her eyes.

She had not wanted to come on this holiday, but Aunt Anne's three younger sisters were grateful to their eldest sister for the way she had stayed at home and looked after their invalid mother, giving them the freedom to marry and raise families, and when she said she needed someone to accompany her on this holiday they had all agreed that a companion would be found. Unfortunately, Lorna seemed to be the only one without previous commitments.

'After all, you said you were owed some holiday and it's not as if you're going anywhere else,' her mother argued.

The clear implication was that not only was Lorna not going anywhere else, but she was also not going *with* anyone else. Lorna's mother was growing worried that at twenty-five Lorna showed no sign of acquiring a steady boyfriend and ignored her daughter's claims that she was perfectly happy devoting herself to her career.

'And your aunt has offered to pay for you,' was her clinching argument.

In the end, it had been easier to agree to come on a fortnight's holiday in Cyprus with Aunt Anne than insist she would rather go walking in the Yorkshire Dales by herself.

Lorna stirred and sat up. It had been a long journey, and she needed a shower. Afterwards, she put on a light dress and had just finished applying lipstick when there was an impatient rap on her door.

'Lorna, are you ready? We've just got time for a drink before dinner.'

★   ★   ★

Downstairs in the high-ceilinged lounge, Aunt Anne looked around as if she was expecting to see familiar faces. Lorna was taken aback when her aunt gave a sudden cry and advanced with hands held out towards an elegant man of indeterminate age whose blazer bore the logo of a firm which specialised in holidays for older people.

'Ben! Are you still here?'

The man smiled and took Aunt Anne's hands in his own.

'Anne! Miss Short! I wasn't expecting to see you.'

Aunt Anne gave an almost girlish giggle.

'Please call me Anne. But I'm afraid I couldn't come with your group this time,' she said regretfully. 'I've come with my niece.'

Lorna became aware of Ben scrutinising her, and realised that, in spite of his general air of amused relaxation, his eyes were observant and penetrating.

'Well, you are both welcome to join in our activities whenever you like,' he offered. 'I think there are some people you know here.' His look focussed on someone across the room. 'Oh, there's Miss Owens. She didn't feel well this morning. I'll just see if she is all right now. See you later.'

Aunt Anne's eyes followed him as he made his way across the room.

'The best travel rep I've ever met,' she said firmly, before heading for two large, comfortable armchairs where she sank down before beckoning a passing waiter.

'Two gin and tonics, please,' she ordered without consulting Lorna.

'I don't usually drink alcohol before dinner,' Lorna informed her, but her aunt waved this information aside.

'You are on holiday. Enjoy yourself. I'm going to.'

She snuggled back into the chair and looked around the lounge with a proprietary air.

'I like this hotel. It feels like coming home.'

Suddenly she leaned forward and waved.

'Coo-ee, Maud!'

A plump woman looked round, waved back, and hurried over.

'Anne! When did you arrive?'

'This afternoon. Is Audrey with you?'

'Of course,' said a voice behind them and another mature lady appeared, beaming. 'How are you? Did you get my card from Egypt?'

In five minutes Aunt Anne was part of a noisy group, all of whom appeared to be old and dear friends, busy exchanging news and gossip. Lorna sat nursing her drink, feeling out of place until, as if at a prearranged signal, the group members rose to their feet.

'Time for dinner, Lorna,' her aunt informed her.

They were greeted at the restaurant

entrance by the head waiter, whose underlings were busy guiding guests to tables, but Aunt Anne waved him firmly aside.

'Ben will find seats for us,' she declared.

Ben was in fact busy steering people gently but firmly into compatible groups and welcomed Aunt Anne and Laura with a wide smile.

'Audrey's on this table. Do you want to sit with her?' he asked, drawing out a chair for Aunt Anne. The head waiter appeared and murmured something before returning to the door. Ben's expression did not alter.

'Lorna? You can sit here next to your aunt.' He turned round. 'That leaves one more seat. Would you like to sit here?'

There was a mumbled reply but Ben was already sliding out the empty chair next to Lorna and somebody was firmly ushered into it. Lorna turned to see who it was and her welcoming smile froze as she recognised the young man she had encountered at the carousel. He, in turn, gave her a horrified look. She forced herself to smile.

'Don't worry. I promise I will do my best not to injure you in any way.'

He managed a fleeting smile.

The meal was an elaborate buffet with guests free to work their way through at least four courses if they wished. Aunt Anne and her friends obviously did wish to do so. Lorna intended to restrict herself to two and managed to resist the seductive desserts. The young man did the same. This left the two of them idly sitting at the table while more determined eaters ate their way through every course. Finally their mutual silence became embarrassing and Lorna turned to him.

'I like your tie,' she remarked.

It was pale gold, divided into small squares which each contained a miniature flower. The young man's hand flew up to it self-consciously.

'Thank you. My sister gave it to me because of my interest in gardening.'

Now the ice was broken he looked round at the other diners before confiding in Lorna.

'I didn't know whether to wear a tie or not. The brochure did say formal wear for dinner.'

'I think that just means you can't wear shorts.' Lorna laughed. 'But you're not alone. There are some other men wearing ties.'

'I saw that. Otherwise mine would be in my pocket by now,' the young man confessed. Then he smiled. 'My name is James Young, by the way.'

'And I'm Lorna Evans. Incidentally, I am sorry for the way I seemed to be continually attacking you earlier. I was feeling a little stressed.'

James grinned and looked past her at Aunt Anne.

'I think I understand.'

There was a rustle on Lorna's left. Apparently it had been decided that the ladies had eaten enough to survive till breakfast and were now preparing to move back to the lounge for coffee.

Lorna automatically followed them and found Ben the rep once again tactfully organising clients into groups who settled into the deep armchairs and couches, and once again Laura found James Young in the next seat. She desperately tried to think of a topic of conversation.

'What kind of gardening are you interested in?' she asked finally.

He considered the question carefully instead of giving a glib response.

'I care about growing things,' he said finally. 'I'm not particularly interested in garden design or the latest fashion in plants. I like to grow healthy vegetables and beautiful flowers.'

'So do you have your own garden?'

'I've got a couple of acres of land altogether, though it is not all garden. I have a small orchard, and some specimen trees. And, of course, there is my workshop. I make handmade furniture.'

'What do you make? Benches, bird tables?'

He looked at her almost with horror.

'No, you don't understand. I don't make garden furniture. I make proper furniture — chairs, dining tables, cupboards — that sort of thing.'

She regarded at him with respect.

'How did you start doing that?'

He shrugged.

'My father was a carpenter, though he worked mostly on repairs. My earliest memory is the smell of freshly-sawn wood and I grew up learning all about the different types of wood and what they should be used for. Then it turned out I had quite a flair for design, so I combined the two interests and started making things. At first it was smallish objects like coffee tables, but people liked them and word spread and I was able to be more ambitious.'

'You have been lucky,' Lorna said enviously.

'I know. I have always felt that you cannot be really happy unless you are doing something you really care about.

Of course, there are drawbacks, especially when you are running a small business. I seem to waste hours filling in forms for the Inland Revenue. They appear to be convinced I must be trying to cheat them out of a little income tax. The whole lot are a pain in the neck.' He looked at her enquiringly. 'What do you do, Lorna?'

She was sitting upright, her lips tightened.

'I am an accountant with the Inland Revenue,' she said crisply.

James gulped, tried to think of something to say, failed, and finally muttered something inarticulate before rising and making for the lifts.

Aunt Anne, who had apparently been deeply immersed in gossip with three other mature ladies, swung round and fixed Lorna with an eagle eye.

'What did you say to that young man? You seem to have scared him off pretty thoroughly.'

'I think he was tired.'

Aunt Anne lifted a disbelieving

eyebrow before turning back to her friends. Lorna sat by silently, wishing she was at home in her flat, until the ladies decided it was time to retire. Alone in her room at last, Lorna prepared herself for bed and settled down to read for a bit before going to sleep, but she could not concentrate. Putting the book down, she brooded on the past day, silently vowing to herself that this would not be the first step on a road that would lead to her becoming the permanent carer for Aunt Anne. As for James Young and his opinion of the Inland Revenue, well! Stupid idiot!

Lorna turned off the light, thumped the pillow into shape and lay down, but did not feel ready for sleep. She knew that many people shared his opinion. Even her mother had not been enthusiastic over her choice of career.

'It sounds a little dull,' she had ventured. 'All numbers, no soul. Wouldn't you rather deal with people?'

In vain Lorna had tried to explain the appeal of numbers, of mathematics, but had failed. Her mother had accepted that it was a necessary job and, importantly, a safe job, but that was all.

'You can't talk to me about it,' she complained.

'Of course not. A lot of it is confidential.'

'Is it ever exciting?'

'Rarely,' Lorna admitted. She had grown accustomed to the way people reacted when she told them she worked for the Inland Revenue, the sudden wary look in their eyes, followed by the well-worn jokes. She herself was growing tired of the ugly, featureless building she worked in and finally fell asleep to dream of working in a garden surrounded by apple trees.

2

Used to getting up early to commute to work, Lorna had to wait for some time before her aunt emerged the next morning. During breakfast she reminded her aunt that their travel rep had called a welcome meeting for half past ten. Aunt Anne shook her head.

'Oh, I told her we wouldn't be coming. I know enough about Paphos and Cyprus already. Remember, I used to come here before the island was divided between the Greeks and the Turks, and I hope to be coming here when the island is united again.'

'But what shall we do about booking excursions? There are some places I want to see but I don't think I would be happy hiring a car.'

'We'll go on Ben's excursions, of course. The coach firms don't mind who comes so long as they pay.'

Suddenly, therefore, the morning was free.

'Shall we walk down to the harbour for a coffee, as you suggested?'

Aunt Anne looked slightly guilty.

'Oh, didn't I tell you that Audrey and I had booked appointments to have our hair done in the salon? Last time I was here they styled it beautifully.'

So the morning was her own, and once Audrey and Aunt Anne had gone off together Lorna collected her book from her room and found a vacant sun lounger. After a while, however, she found that she was neglecting the book in order to speculate why had Aunt Anne insisted on bringing a companion when she had apparently been expecting to meet old friends and did not seem to need Lorna's assistance for anything. Maybe Lorna was an expensive 'just in case'. So while she waited for any unexpected emergency, she was free to lounge in the sun between large, well-cooked meals. There were worse fates. However, she knew herself well enough to know that such inactivity would rapidly bore her. She wanted to explore the area, to see what Cyprus had to offer, but in a strange country that was best done with a companion. Was there any group she could join, anyone she could make friends with?

She started to observe the rest of the guests who were around the pool or wandering through the gardens, and gradually became aware of the fact that virtually none of them were under fifty years old. Of course, the school holidays were over, so there were no families, and not many young people of her age could afford the Hotel Persepolis. Ben's clients definitely predominated. She did see one young couple but they had eyes only for each other and she decided that they were on their honeymoon and would not want a third person tagging along with them.

Finally Lorna let her eyes close and drifted off into a gentle doze. After a while she was awoken by the creak of the neighbouring sun lounger as someone lowered themselves on it. She looked across and saw James Young sitting on the edge looking at her.

'Okay,' he said without preamble. 'You hurt my leg and then I hurt your feelings. Can we call it quits and make a fresh start?'

There was no smile, no persuasive grin. He sat looking at her directly, his face serious.

'Why?' Lorna returned baldly.

He waved a hand at the scene.

'Because we are the only two people here under fifty, as far as I can see, so who else are we going to talk to? I'm here on my own. You are here with an aunt who seems to have plenty of friends of her own age. Are we going to spend the next two weeks sitting by ourselves, bored stiff?'

Lorna rapidly made up her mind.

'Mr Young, I forgive you for your low opinion of the Inland Revenue and I hope your bruises are fading. What shall we talk about?'

Now a grin did appear and James

Young relaxed visibly.

'Tell me what you would like to drink first.'

Lying back, enjoying a fresh orange juice, Lorna inspected her companion. He looked about thirty, with untidy fair hair and a face that was pleasant rather than handsome. She noticed his large, capable hands and the tan which showed he must spend a lot of time out of doors.

'Why are you here on your own? As we've both noticed, it's not really a place for people our age,' she said curiously.

'I didn't know anything about the hotel or Cyprus when I booked. I just realised suddenly that I hadn't had a break for two years, so I went to the local travel agent and asked them to recommend somewhere comfortable for a couple of weeks, and this is what they sold me.'

'Why couldn't you take a holiday before?'

He sipped his own drink, obviously marshalling his thoughts. This was not a man who rushed into speech.

'I told you I make handmade furniture. I've been doing that for years, but I wasn't earning enough from that, so I was a jobbing carpenter, as well as a part-time gardener when anyone wanted any work done. I used to mow the lawns for a woman who told a friend about me and my furniture. He was an interior designer.'

'Anyway, he came to see my work, liked it, bought everything I had for sale and commissioned some more. He told his clients and friends about me and suddenly I was a success with more work than I could cope with. During the last two years I've taken people on, trained them, set up a website, learned to market what I make.' His rare grin reappeared. 'One of the things the interior designer told me — after he'd bought all my stuff — was that I was charging far too little for my products. It has been a very busy but rewarding time, and the business is going well now.'

He looked at her challengingly.

'Now it's your turn. Tell me about the attractions of the Inland Revenue.'

'It does have some,' she protested. 'It's steady, useful work. You can't run the country without taxes.' His face was carefully blank. 'All right, I didn't wake up one day and decide that I wanted to be an accountant. But at school I loved mathematics, and there didn't seem to be many other jobs which required them, except teaching, and I don't think I could face a classroom full of kids and try to explain trigonometry to them. Teaching takes courage.' There was a wistful expression on her face. 'It sounds as if your work makes you happy; I'm satisfied with mine, so far.'

'I have been very lucky,' he conceded. 'I love the work I do. I live in a beautiful little town, and I have a large, supportive family. I think my mother had dreams of me working in an office and wearing a suit, but once she saw that making things was what I really wanted to do, that it made me happy, she accepted it.'

'My family seem to think that the job I am doing is just to fill in time till I get married,' Lorna complained. 'They don't seem to realise that, actually, I am doing quite well.'

'And are you planning to get married soon?'

Lorna shook her head. 'I've had boyfriends, but so far I haven't met anyone I liked enough to spend the rest of my life with.'

'My trouble is that girls want someone with a bit more polish than me, someone who hasn't always got sawdust in his clothes,' James said resignedly. 'Well, I expect I'll meet someone who wants to take care of me and tidy me up sometime.'

A brisk voice interrupted them.

'Have you been sitting here all morning? Your nose is getting quite red, you know, Lorna.'

Aunt Anne, fresh from the hairdresser, demanded admiration of her new hair style before sweeping Lorna off to lunch.

'Are you coming?' Lorna asked James, but he shook his head, heaving himself to his feet.

'I'm here on half-board, so I am going to find a cafe and have a snack. I'll probably see you later.'

'He seems quite a pleasant young man,' Aunt Anne observed, watching his retreating figure.

3

As they finished lunch Lorna, as befitted a good niece, asked her aunt what she wanted to do that afternoon. Aunt Anne yawned.

'Well, I'm going to have coffee and then a nap, of course. Then Audrey and I are going to play bridge with a couple of other ladies. That should take us up to the time to shower and change for dinner.'

'And what am I supposed to do?' Lorna enquired sweetly.

Her aunt gave her a sharp look and pursed her lips.

'Lorna, I think it is time we had a talk. Go and find us a quiet table in the lounge while I order coffee.'

They settled in a remote corner and Aunt Anne faced Lorna.

'First of all, let me clear up a few misapprehensions your family may have given you about me. I know they see me as a lonely, unfulfilled elderly spinster who sacrificed herself to look after her sick mother.' A rather wicked grin appeared briefly. 'Maybe I have encouraged that view of me, but the truth is that, on the whole, I have been very satisfied with my life. When I was young I did care for a man, and I think he cared for me, but he was killed in an accident before we even had a chance to decide whether we loved each other or not.'

'After that, I was perfectly happy to stay single. I never particularly wanted children, and being unmarried meant I had a lot more freedom. I had a career I enjoyed and your grandmother didn't need full-time care till it was time for me to retire anyway. As a result, I am comfortable financially. I am also healthy. There is absolutely no reason for you to feel sorry for me or fuss round me.'

Lorna considered this statement. 'Then why am I here?' she said at last.

For the first time her aunt looked uncertain.

'I suppose there is no nice way of putting this, Lorna. I felt sorry for you.' As Lorna sat upright and glared at her indignantly, Aunt Anne held up her hand. 'Listen to me, and then you can say what you like. Even as a child you were obviously very bright and academically promising. But then you became one of those unfortunate teenagers who go through a physically awkward time. You had bad skin. You were always eating to compensate for feeling unattractive so you ended up spotty *and* overweight. As a result you lost all your self-confidence and you never seem to have regained it properly. You are now a slim and attractive young woman, but I sense that every time you look in the mirror you still see that unfortunate teenager.'

'So you don't have the confidence to take risks. You took a safe job, and although you are doing quite well in it, I'm not sure it really satisfies you or uses all your talents. You wear safe clothes. You never do anything to your hair or use make-up that could draw attention to you. Your boyfriends have been safe, reliable and dull. So I decided you needed to be taken away from your usual surroundings and given a chance to think about whether there is anything you would really like to do to fulfil your potential. That is why you are here. You have a fortnight to sit and think about your life and where you are going. If you decide that you want to continue doing what you are doing now, then no harm is done. If you decide you want to take a chance, to try something new, then let me know and I will help you if I can. That's all.'

Lorna found she had nothing to say and her aunt rose.

'Well, I'll go and have my nap now. See you before dinner.'

Lorna remained seated for a while until she realised that she was blinking away tears. She did not yet feel grateful for her aunt's frankness or the opportunity she was giving her. All she could think of was that her aunt was sorry for her! She was an object of pity! She sprang to her feet and made for the hotel's main door, feeling that she needed to walk somewhere to work off her feelings. Outside the hotel, she turned left and began to walk down towards the harbour. After a while, she realised that there were footsteps keeping pace with hers and looked up to see James Young beside her.

'I saw you leave the hotel and I thought you might like a companion,' he said awkwardly, 'but it looks as though you have a problem. Can I help?'

Lorna shook her head, sniffed, searched for a tissue in her bag and blew her nose loudly.

'I don't think so. I'm angry, but I can't discuss the reason why with you.' She gave a half-laugh. 'If you were a girl I could discuss it with you and you could give me advice.'

'Oh, *that* kind of problem! I'm afraid I can't be a female confidante, but at least let me walk to the harbour with you and buy you a cup of coffee.'

It would have been rude to reject his offer, so Lorna nodded and they strode downhill in silence, but it was undeniably comforting to have someone beside her. When they reached the harbour, they found people strolling along in the sunshine with a row of restaurants and souvenir shops and chairs and tables set out by the waterside waiting for the tourists who needed refreshment or a rest. Lorna was gazing with interest at a girl teetering along on six-inch heels, wondering how she managed to avoid breaking an ankle, when she heard a strange sound from James. Startled, she turned round and found him staring at a display of souvenirs which included an olivewood carving of a mermaid and a dolphin engaged in some mildly scandalous behaviour.

'Look at that!' James exploded, pointing furiously at the carving. 'They take that beautiful wood and turn it into a monstrosity! Look at the grain! If they had taken the trouble they could have used the wood to make something lovely that would be cherished for generations! As it is, can you imagine anything more ugly?'

He was red-faced and beginning to wave his arms about. As the shop's owner advanced towards them, Lorna seized James' sleeve and pulled him away, leading him to a table by the water a safe distance from the shop. She ordered two coffees and waited until James had calmed down.

'I'm sorry,' he said finally, 'but I care about beautiful wood.'

'You made that clear. If it is any comfort, I don't think anyone will buy that object. It is too ugly.' She laughed. 'I thought you were going to pick it up and smash it!'

He was not listening.

'If I had found that bit of wood I wouldn't have tried to carve it into a figure at all. I would have made an abstract shape, gently curving, so that people would have wanted to touch it and stroke it.'

Lorna looked at him with new respect. Here was a man who was not only a craftsman, clearly talented with his hands, but an artist, too.

They drank their coffee, looking at the harbour which sheltered boats ranging from elegant yachts to small fishing vessels.

'Thank you for stopping me making too much of a spectacle of myself,' James said finally. 'Are you quite sure there is nothing I can do to help you in return?'

'Quite sure . . . ' She paused. 'Maybe there is one thing. As a designer, what do you think of my hairstyle?'

He sat back and inspected her, his eyes narrowed and his lips thinned as he looked at her mid-brown hair, parted on one side and cut just above her shoulders. It was easy to care for and she thought it disguised her long neck.

James sat forward, his mind made up.

'You could do better,' he pronounced. 'As it is, it is shapeless and rather unbecoming. You should have it cut short to show off the shape of your head. And you've got a lovely, elegant neck. It's a pity to hide it.'

Shocked, Lorna glared at him.

'I like my hair as it is.'

James brushed this aside.

'Then why ask me? Anyway, trust me. I know about shapes.' Then, as she continued to glare, he wilted slightly. 'I suppose there is nothing actually wrong with it as it is. It is a safe style.'

This echo of her aunt was too much. Lorna's fingers tightened on her cup until her knuckles whitened.

'Don't throw that cup at me,' James said hastily. 'If you didn't want my advice, you shouldn't have asked for it.'

Lorna released her grip on the cup and forced a smile.

'It's my turn to say sorry. Neither of us is at our best this afternoon.'

James thrust back his chair.

'Let's forgive each other, yet again, and do a bit more sightseeing.'

Turning away from the harbour they

found Paphos's main claim to fame, a world-famous area which had once been covered with stately Roman houses. The floors, many of them decorated with elaborate mosaics, had been declared a World Heritage Site. Lorna and James wandered along the paths connecting the various excavations, admiring the views over the sea rather than the archaeological remains. It was very soothing.

James turned his back on the sea and looked inland to where the Troodos Mountains reared skywards.

'That's where I'd like to go. I should think there are some magnificent views up there.'

'Aunt Anne says there is an excursion into the mountains which takes you to a monastery.'

He grimaced. 'I want to see the mountains. The landscape, the scenery . . . not a monastery.'

'Apparently there are still monks there, so you have to be careful what you wear,' Lorna continued.

He glanced at her.

'Well, you won't shock them.'

Lorna bit her lip. So her clothes were 'safe' as well as her hair!

'Shall we go back?' she said abruptly. 'I've seen enough for now.'

It was an easy, ten minute walk back up the hill to the hotel and neither of them spoke. Once inside the cool reception area, Lorna halted, uncertain how to part.

'Thank you for your company,' she said formally, and then smiled. 'I enjoyed the harbour. We may not exactly bring out the best in each other, but it was fun, even so.'

He smiled, nodding his agreement.

'Perhaps we can explore somewhere else together.'

Before she had a chance to give him an answer Katerina, the receptionist, hurried up to her.

'Miss Evans? Your aunt left a message with me. In case you are looking for her, she has gone out with a friend, but she said to tell you she will be back in time for dinner.'

'Thank you,' Lorna said, and turned to find that James had gone. She took the lift to her room, ready for a short rest before a shower, but before she lay down she stood in front of the full-length mirror on the wall and tried to look at herself objectively.

It was true that she had left her teenage difficulties behind and that now her figure was slim and her skin free from blemishes. Lorna viewed herself from various angles. She was perfectly presentable. Exciting? No. There was nothing about her to make anyone take a second look, but that was what she had aimed for. She didn't want to stand out, to be conspicuous. As a result her appearance was, she had to admit, a little dull, what her aunt had described as 'safe'. Still looking in the mirror, she lifted her hair up to ear level, frowned at the result and let it fall back into place. Then she stuck out her tongue at her reflection and settled herself on her bed with a book.

She was woken some time later by the sound of excited voices outside her door. She got up to open it and saw Aunt Anne and her friend Audrey struggling to open her aunt's door with their arms full of parcels.

'Oh, Lorna, I'm glad you're awake. Can you take my key and open the door? We've been to a new shopping mall and I think we got carried away.'

Lorna thought of the heavy case her aunt had brought and decided she would need another to get her purchases home.

'Don't forget we'll all be doing more shopping tomorrow,' Audrey reminded her before departing for her own room.

'Tomorrow? What is happening tomorrow?'

Aunt Anne, busy checking her parcels, looked up briefly and smiled sweetly.

'Oh, I've signed us both up for an excursion to Curium. It is a beautiful Roman amphitheatre.'

'Are there shops there?'

'Of course not! The shops are in a

village we call at first. Apparently the women make lace and the men do silverwork. We'll be able to buy plenty of souvenirs, so I thought you would like to go.'

Lorna closed the door quietly behind her and returned to her own room. Culture and shopping combined — well, it could be fun . . .

4

Certainly it was fun — though not terribly exciting. Lorna bought two silver bracelets and four cushion covers, ate with pleasure the lunch they were served in a taverna, and admired the Roman remains. The coach returned to the hotel about four o'clock and Ben was waiting to greet his charges with a smile.

'Did you enjoy yourselves?' he enquired.

Heads nodded and there were contented murmurs, but just as Ben was turning away, satisfied that all was well, Aunt Anne spoke up.

'There was one thing . . . I noticed it first when we were driving here from the airport . . . There seem to be new houses being built everywhere — hundreds of them.'

Ben focussed on her regretfully.

'I know, Miss Short. The trouble is, farmers have been having a bad time what with droughts and various EU regulations, so many of them have decided to cut their losses or go for a quick profit and they have sold their land to speculative developers. The developers are building houses as fast as they can to sell to foreigners, often as holiday homes.'

'But they are ruining the landscape in several places we saw.'

'I know,' Ben agreed, 'and I think they may be heading for trouble by being too greedy. Already they are finding it difficult to sell what they are building. Now, forget them and come and have a cup of tea.'

Aunt Anne made for the lifts and her room, but Lorna excused herself. There was something she wanted to do first. After completing her mission, she wandered out into the sunshine and found James Young drowsing on a sun lounger. He stirred and opened his eyes as she sat down next to him. Recognising her, he struggled to a sitting position.

'Had a good day?' he enquired.

'It was very pleasant. And you?'

'I have been a good holidaymaker. I have swum, walked along the beach, sunbathed, swum again, and then sunbathed again. Very relaxing for a day, but a fortnight of it could get a bit boring.'

'So what are you going to do?'

'I have plans,' he said smugly, but did not add any more, and Lorna went off to take her purchases to her room.

That evening, after dinner, a trio of musicians was playing music intended to tempt the guests to dance after they had finished their coffees and liqueurs. The music was smooth, most of it tunes from a few decades ago. A few couples did get up to exhibit their ballroom dancing skills, but there was still plenty of space left on the dance floor. Then as it grew late the tempo changed. A hint of jazz could be detected. The dancers hesitated, a little unsure, and then began to move a bit more freely.

James, who had been sitting silently next to Lorna, suddenly stretched out a hand to her.

'Come on,' he said. 'They're playing our music now.'

Lorna hesitated. She knew she was not a good dancer, always afraid of forgetting the steps.

'Go on, Lorna!' her aunt urged.

Lorna decided it would be difficult to refuse and obediently stood up and let James take her on to the floor, but the first couple of minutes were as bad as she had feared. She felt stiff and clumsy, unable to move to the rhythm of the music, but then she found that James was adapting his movements to hers so that he compensated for her awkwardness. As a result she began to relax, and by the end of the dance was actually enjoying herself. As the music finished she prepared to leave the floor, but James held on to her hand, detaining her.

'Another dance,' he insisted.

Now the music was faster, freer.

'I don't know what to do,' she said in sudden panic.

'Do what your body tells you to do,'

he instructed her, spinning her round so that her skirt belled out.

It might have been the music or the unfamiliar surroundings which freed her from her inhibitions, but Lorna obeyed him, letting the music dictate her movements, guided by his deft touches when she faltered, in tune with the movements of his body. The music ended to the sound of applause and Lorna realised that all the other dancers had left the floor and together with the guests in the lounge had formed an audience for the pair of them. She blushed vividly and made for her seat, acknowledging the compliments they received with a nervous nod. Aunt Anne regarded her with surprised approval.

'I didn't know you could dance like that, Lorna,' she commented.

'Neither did I, but I had a good partner.'

James Young grinned.

'I couldn't have done it if you hadn't had the ability in you.'

James left soon afterwards, claiming

that he always went to bed early. Lorna also pleaded fatigue so that she could enjoy a little solitude in her own room. Aunt Anne seemed set for the evening and Lorna was fast asleep when her aunt finally came upstairs.

★   ★   ★

The next morning, Lorna slipped away from her aunt after breakfast and went to keep the appointment she had made the previous afternoon. Her heart was beating fast as she took her seat in the hairdresser's salon.

'I would like my hair cut shorter,' she instructed the neat little woman who bustled up to take charge of her. 'Not too short,' she added hastily, her courage failing.

The hairdresser walked round her slowly, viewing her from every angle.

'Cutting it short would help,' she pronounced finally, 'but you should also have your parting moved. And your hair needs layering, of course. Leave it to me.'

She picked up her scissors and advanced. After five minutes, horrified by the amount of hair falling to the floor, Lorna closed her eyes and resolved not to look again until the whole process was finished. If it looked too dreadful, she would just have to wait till it grew again.

Finally, after what seemed a very long time, the hairdresser said 'There!' in a satisfied tone.

'You may look now,' she instructed.

Lorna opened her eyes, gazed in the mirror, and tried not to burst into tears. Her head looked tiny, her neck a yard long.

'It suits you,' pronounced the hairdresser before producing a large bill. Lorna paid her and fled. Head bent, desperately making for the shelter of her room, she bumped into someone.

'Are you attacking me again?' James Young said resignedly. Then he looked at her and his face lit up. 'You've had your hair cut!'

He stood back, regarding her with his

head on one side while she wondered if she could dart past him, and then he nodded decisively.

'It looks really, really good! Your face isn't hidden under a shapeless mass any longer.'

'It looks dreadful! And it's all your fault! You told me to get it cut.'

'And I was right! Remember, I know about shape and balance. Shake your head.'

She found herself obeying him.

'See? It falls back into place beautifully,' he said triumphantly.

Lorna sought reassurance.

'Do you really think it looks all right? I was horrified when I saw it.'

'You probably haven't done anything adventurous to your hair for years. I assure you that it suits you perfectly. Let us go and see what your aunt thinks of it.'

James took her by the elbow and steered her on to the sun terrace where Aunt Anne could be seen sitting with a group of cronies. As the two of them approached, Aunt Anne looked up, stared at them, blinked twice, and then stared again.

'Lorna, what have you done to your hair?' She saw her niece's thunderous expression and added hastily, 'It looks marvellous!'

The other ladies joined in the chorus of praise, a couple of them asking where she had had it done. Their admiration was obviously genuine and Lorna was finally able to relax and even to smile.

'Now you should try a different colour,' her aunt pronounced.

'Dye my hair?' Lorna answered in horror, feeling that would definitely be a step too far.

'Not dye it, my dear. Try a rinse. Just enhance it a little.'

The suggestion produced another animated discussion among the ladies till Lorna told them she was going up to her room. James was waiting for her in a quiet corner.

'I was right, wasn't I?'

'Apparently. I am going to go and

stare in the mirror for ten minutes.' She looked at him accusingly. 'Well, I've taken one positive step. What about you.'

He smiled, held out a clenched fist and opened it. In his hand lay a set of car keys.

'I've hired a car. Meet me in reception at two o'clock and I will take you for a test drive.'

Well, it would be one way to pass an afternoon which her aunt had announced she would be devoting to bridge, so promptly at two o'clock Lorna was waiting at the hotel's main door. James arrived, switched off the engine and got out.

'What do you think?'

Lorna walked round the vehicle, noting every scratch and spot of rust.

'You said you'd hired a car. This is a jeep. A very old jeep.'

James looked rather offended, Lorna decided. Perhaps she'd offended him.

'It's not all that old.' He patted the bonnet fondly. 'It's just like one I had for years. I drove it till it fell to pieces.'

'Are you sure this isn't the same one?'

He shrugged.

'I'll admit it isn't glossy and it doesn't look very beautiful, but it is in good working order. I checked it thoroughly.' Lorna was still looking dubious. 'Look, you don't want a flashy car when you are driving through the mountains in Cyprus. This is sturdy and business-like and it will tackle rough roads. Now, do you want to come with me or not?'

'Have you got a mobile phone with you and have you got the number of the car rental office?'

'Yes.'

'Then I'll risk it,' she said resignedly.

At least in Cyprus they drove on the left, the same side as in England, and the roads were quiet. Lorna began to relax. Then James turned off the main road onto a much narrower road that snaked round curves as the land rose towards the hills.

'Where are you going?'

'I don't know, but there's a map in the glove compartment.'

Lorna found the map, managed to locate the minor road, and told James there was a small village a few miles ahead. They found the village, built on a steep hillside, and negotiated the narrow streets with great care. Then houses became few and far between and the hills were covered with pine woods instead of fields.

'The map isn't very detailed,' Lorna said nervously. 'I'm not sure where we're going now.'

'I'll just go on a bit further, then I'll try to get back a different way.'

This involved taking a road which rapidly degenerated into a track in the woods. James took a right turn.

'I'm not at all sure this is right,' Lorna said breathlessly, being shaken about by the rough surface as she tried to make sense of the map. Then, suddenly, her eyes widened.

'Stop!' she cried out.

James braked abruptly.

'What's the matter?'

'We're driving down a river bed,' Lorna informed him through gritted teeth. 'Reverse now.'

It took some careful manoeuvring, but the jeep regained the road intact and James agreed to retrace their route. Safely back at the hotel, Lorna climbed stiffly out of the jeep.

'I need a gin and tonic,' she announced.

'Find a seat while I get us both one,' James replied with a warm smile.

Lorna found a large, comfortable seat and sank into it gratefully.

'You have to admit the jeep survived. It even managed a river bed,' James argued as they drank.

'Okay, I'll give you that. What on earth do you drive at home?'

'I've got a light van and a lorry. That's what I need for moving furniture and wood.' He frowned. 'Come to think of it, I haven't ever had an proper car. What about you?'

'My father has a saloon. If I need a

car, I borrow that.'

He nodded politely.

'Very sensible. Now, where do you want to go tomorrow?'

'Somewhere flat! We could go north of Paphos, to Aphrodite's Bath.'

He frowned.

'The Troodos Mountains are really spectacular.'

'You said you'd hired the jeep for the rest of your holiday. We could go up into the mountains another day,' Lorna argued. 'And I've got a guide to Cyprus which shows the route to Aphrodite's Bath very clearly.'

James submitted with fairly good grace.

'We'll set off after breakfast and have lunch somewhere. If we take our cameras we should get some good pictures.'

'Then that's agreed.' She rose, feeling as if she were creaking audibly. 'Now I am going to have a hot bath and inspect my bruises . . . '

5

She was dressing after her bath when her aunt knocked on her door. 'Where have you been?' her aunt demanded.

'I told you I was going for a drive with James — with Mr Young.'

Her aunt thumped herself down in the only armchair.

'You might have found me to tell me you were back,' Aunt Anne said fretfully. 'When I said I didn't want you around me all the time, I didn't mean I wanted you to abandon me completely. I wanted to spend time with you, too.'

'What's the matter?' Lorna said sharply. 'I thought you would enjoy a bridge afternoon.'

Aunt Anne sniffed audibly.

'Enjoyment depends on who you are playing with and how they are playing. Tomorrow I think I would like the two of us to take the bus to Upper Paphos.'

Tomorrow? But that would mean she couldn't go out with James. She was about to explain that she would not be free the following day, but then told herself that she should put her aunt's requirements first. After all, she was paying for Lorna's holiday. And there was always the chance that Aunt Anne would change her mind if she had a good evening.

Lorna decided to change the subject.

'You know, I'm getting used to this hairstyle. It does suit me. I'll have to thank James for suggesting it.'

Her aunt's eyebrows rose.

'You've only known him a couple of days and you are taking his advice on how you do your hair? As well as spending all your time with him? You don't want him thinking you are throwing yourself at him.'

Lorna's self-confidence, always feeble, began to drain away. James had seemed to enjoy her company, but perhaps her aunt was right. Perhaps he had only asked her out as a matter of politeness, or because he felt pity for her, tagging along after her aunt. The idea was humiliating. Well, she would let fate decide whether she would be going out with her aunt or with James.

Lorna avoided James at dinner, managing to sit at a table with no other vacant seat. It was cowardly, but she did still have a lingering hope that something would rescue her day out with him. After all, there was a limit to politeness and he would not have asked her to go with him if he had been bored by her or thought her over-eager.

Later that evening she realised that Ben was standing near the quiet corner where she had retreated with a book.

'Did you want to see me?' she asked. 'Is it something about my aunt?'

'Just a minor point,' he said smiling, taking the seat opposite. 'I wondered if you had noticed that Miss Short was not in a very good mood this evening.'

'She did seem a little upset about something,' Lorna said slowly.

Ben leant forward and patted her hand.

'Good news. Your aunt has been restored to her usual happy frame of mind.'

'What was the matter?'

'I understand you don't play bridge, so you wouldn't understand. Let us say that there was a slight misunderstanding which I cleared up by producing a copy of the rules of the game.'

She looked at him with respect.

'You know, Ben, you are a very good rep.'

'I try to be. It helps if you have an incurable curiosity about people.'

He left, and soon after her aunt, passing by with Maud, informed her casually that she had changed her mind and would not need her company the next day. When James appeared a minute later, Lorna began to feel that her 'quiet corner' was more like a thoroughfare.

'I wanted to ask you if it would be all right if we left about ten tomorrow,' he said pleasantly.

Lorna might not have to worry about

her aunt any more, but she wanted to make absolutely sure that James really wanted her company. She bit her lip.

'I've been thinking about that. Perhaps it would be better if I didn't come with you. Then you can go where you want.'

He sat down opposite her.

'What's the matter?'

'Nothing. I just thought you might prefer it that way.'

'Then you were wrong. I enjoyed our trip out today and I will enjoy going to other places more if you're with me.'

'In that case, I'll be ready at ten o'clock.' She smiled, pleased and flattered.

It looked as if the next day would be a long one, so Lorna decided to go to bed early. On her way to the lifts she passed the reception desk, where Katerina was chatting with one of the assistant managers. She smiled at Lorna.

'I like your new hairstyle, Miss Evans.'

Lorna patted her head.

'So do I. I like your hairdresser and I like your hotel. In fact, I like Cyprus!'

In her room she checked her text messages. There was only one, from her parents, hoping that she was enjoying herself, and that Aunt Anne was not being too demanding. She replied that she was very happy and that Aunt Anne was no trouble at all.

* * *

Aunt Anne was happy to see Lorna go, even mildly apologetic about her previous evening's fit of bad temper.

'I'm sorry, my dear. Bridge does tend to bring out the worst in people. Go and enjoy yourself.'

Lorna set out with that intention. The first part of the journey took them northwards along a main road through the Akamas peninsular. There were occasional spectacular views, but the landscape seemed harsh and barren and there were very few signs of habitation.

'It doesn't look very welcoming,' she ventured.

'The guide describes it as infertile and windswept,' James informed her. 'However, it does have rare plants and animals, and part of it is a national forest. I was thinking of trying to reach Lara Bay,' he said hopefully. 'The sea turtles are protected there.'

Lorna regarded him suspiciously — she knew what he was planning to do.

'Is there a good road to this bay?' he asked as Lorna sat back in her seat.

'To Aphrodite's Bath,' she said firmly.

Once they reached the north coast of the peninsular they turned left and followed the coast. Occasionally a small town offered cafés and shops, or an incongruous hotel sat isolated on a lonely stretch of beach, but they carried on to their destination, which Lorna secretly found a little disappointing. A small pool, shaded by overhanging rocks, Aphrodite's Bath could obviously be a charming spot when it was quiet or deserted, but unfortunately Lorna and James arrived at the same time as two tourist excursion coaches and were forced to walk in single file around the site while dozens of cameras dutifully recorded the scene.

'Apparently if you drink the water from the spring, you will fall in love.'

James offered this nugget of information which Lorna dismissed scornfully. However, when she was sure he was not looking, she surreptitiously dipped one finger in the water and licked it. Maybe that would conjure up a mild flirtation when she got home.

They lunched near the site at a cheerful little café, sitting outside at a sunlit table.

'Where shall we go now?' James asked.

Because the journey there had been so straightforward, they had made good time and there was still a long afternoon to fill. James pointed to a spot on the map.

'Pegeia is said to be very interesting.

There are some early Byzantine churches there, and we can take a major road and eventually get back to Paphos that way,' he tempted her.

Lorna leaned over the map.

'The major road only goes halfway. Then there is a very wiggly minor road, and wiggles mean bends climbing up hills,' she pointed out. She lifted her head. 'You seem to have been doing some research into this area.'

'I mentioned at the hotel reception that we were coming this way and one of the staff who comes from this area was telling me all about it.' He looked at her pleadingly. 'Come on, Lorna. You wanted to see Cyprus away from the tourist resorts and this is your opportunity. I promise I won't drive down any more river beds!'

She laughed and gave in, reminding herself that she was supposed to be trying to be adventurous on this holiday.

★ ★ ★

Later, neither of them could decide who had been responsible, but some distance after the main road to Pegeia it became apparent that somehow they had headed in the wrong direction. The road had suddenly narrowed and was gouged out of the side of a hill.

'Well, this road must go somewhere,' James argued. 'If we go on, we should come to a village or something and then we can find out where we are.'

This seemed logical, and as they drove slowly on, the hillside grew less steep, and suddenly Lorna pointed.

'There! There's a sign to a house or a village. Go that way.'

Obediently James swung the wheel. The track they were following was clear and looked as if it was used frequently. Fields of olive trees and other crops began to appear. Finally they turned a corner and found themselves facing a farmhouse sheltered by a cluster of tall trees. The two-storey stone-built house was long and low with a dark tiled roof, a wing on one end creating an L-shape.

An open balcony that ran the length of the first floor was all that broke the plainness of the grey façade. The heavy wooden door was shut. James prepared to get out of the jeep.

'I'll see if any one is around,' he told Lorna, but before his feet touched the ground, a figure came round the corner of the house. It was a young man of about twenty, casually dressed, who advanced towards them.

'Excuse me,' James called, 'but I'm afraid we are lost . . . '

'English! Tourists!' the young man interrupted him, making an exaggerated bow. 'Welcome! What a pity you didn't wait till next year, then we could have offered you suitable accommodation, a club house, a swimming-pool . . . '

'Demetrius!' Now it was the young man's turn to be interrupted, this time by a girl in jeans and a T-shirt who had followed him round the corner. 'Behave yourself and don't be rude to strangers.'

The young man gave her a furious

look and retreated out of sight while the girl came towards them.

'I must apologise for my brother,' she said. 'He is young and still rather stupid at times. How can I help you?' She stopped and her eyes widened. 'Miss Evans, Mr Young!'

By now Lorna had recognised the girl. It was Katerina, the receptionist from the Hotel Persepolis, looking very different from the trim, uniformed figure she presented at the hotel.

'Katerina, we're glad to see you!' James, now safely on the ground, advanced and took the girl's hands in his, smiling down at her. 'Miss Evans and I are hopelessly lost. We were trying to get to Pegeia but we have no idea where we are now.'

'You are at my home,' Katerina told him, 'and you are very welcome. Come in and rest and I will tell you how to get to Pegeia. It is easy to get lost in these hills.'

She was leading them round the corner when they had to jump aside as a motor bike roared out past them with the young man riding it. Katerina looked after him ruefully, shaking her head, before continuing on her way.

It soon became obvious that, like many rural dwellings, most activity took place at the rear of the house. A kitchen table with chairs around it stood on the cobbled yard and Katerina had clearly been preparing vegetables on it. She swept the onions and carrots to one side and gestured to invite Lorna and James to sit down.

'Let me get you a drink,' she offered. 'Would you like coffee, wine, or a glass of beer?'

Soon she reappeared with cool glasses of the beer they had chosen and sank down gracefully into one of the chairs. She had brought a map which was very like their own, but several extra routes had been added in ink.

'You probably went to the right here, instead of to the left,' she indicated. 'Now, if you go back about two miles, then go to the right, there is a narrow but perfectly safe track that will soon join the road to Pegeia.'

They thanked her sincerely and were just about to drain their glasses and take their leave when another man strode into the courtyard. Dark-haired and muscular, he looked to be in his early thirties, and his deeply tanned face was set in a ferocious frown.

He stopped at the sight of the unexpected visitors and Katerina hurriedly introduced him.

'This is Andreas, my other brother. Andreas, Miss Evans and Mr Young are staying at the hotel. They got lost and ended up here.'

The frown vanished and white teeth showed in her brother's face. Suddenly he was a charming and rather attractive young man.

'That is not uncommon.' Then he turned back to Katerina. 'Do you know where Demetrius is? I want him to help me with the balcony.'

'He's just ridden off.'

'When will he be back?'

'He didn't say.'

The frown returned.

'Well, I can't do it by myself. The wood has to be cut to a precise size and then fitted into place. It needs two of us.'

James's face had lit up.

'Can I help you?' he enquired.

Andreas looked at him politely but a little dismissively.

'Only if you know something about carpentry.'

James's smile grew wider and he stood up.

'Andreas, you don't know it yet, but you are in luck. Now, show me what you want done.'

When James had gone off with a rather reluctant Andreas, Katerina turned apologetically to Lorna.

'I am afraid you have been deserted. What would you like to do?'

'First of all I would like to help you finish preparing those vegetables, and then perhaps you could show me round a bit.'

As they chopped and diced, Lorna asked Katerina how she reconciled the two very different sides of her life — living in an isolated farm and working in a highly sophisticated tourist hotel. Katerina shrugged.

'I like both places. I probably like them more because they are so different. The farm is my home and it's quiet and peaceful and I love the animals and also growing things. But I also love the glamour and comfort of the hotel and meeting all the different people.'

'Isn't it difficult to reach Paphos from here?'

'Not really. I can take the short cuts on my moped or sometimes Demetrius gives me a lift on his bike. He is at college, studying tourism.' She suddenly fell quiet and Lorna waited a little before asking her next question.

'What did he mean by saying there would be a clubhouse and swimming pool here next year? Are you selling the farm?'

Katerina shook her head violently.

'No! Not if Andreas and I can stop it!'

There were tears in her eyes and Lorna hurried to apologise for upsetting her, but the girl put down her knife and managed a watery smile.

'After the way Demetrius behaved, you have a right to know. My father died suddenly last year, without leaving a will, so all four of his children have inherited an equal share. Andreas has never wanted to do anything but live here and work the farm. This is my family home and it would break my heart to see it sold and tacky little chalets built on it. But Demetrius is young and doesn't want to be tied to the land. He has friends at college whose fathers have made a lot of money by dealing in land and building for tourists. He wants to sell the farm, take the money and move to a city.'

'You said there were four children.'

'There is my sister Agnes. She is married with two young children, and although she is fond of the farm, she would like some extra money.' She blew her nose loudly. 'Even if Andreas and I refuse to sell, if the other two sell their shares half the land would not be a viable farm, but, then again, half might not be enough for a tourist development.' She sighed. 'Each night Demetrius is urging us to sell, and then he and Andreas argue. There are many local people who support us, who have seen what has happened in tourist resorts and don't want it to happen here.'

She stood up resolutely.

'That is enough of our troubles. Now, when I have put these on the stove I am going to find out what has happened to my brother and Mr Young.'

In fact there was no need to go looking for the two men as a clatter of shoes on wooden stairs could be clearly heard and the two emerged into the sunlight smiling, clearly very pleased with each other.

'Your friend is a craftsman!' Andreas informed Lorna. 'He knew exactly what wanted doing. I thought it would take two hours at least to mend that section.'

'I told you that instead of adding bits at random, it was just a case of working out how the men who made it intended it to go together. But you will have to see to that other stretch soon or it will be dangerous.'

'Come back and help me do it.'

James, pleased and flattered, assured Andreas that he would do that. Lorna felt grimly that her chances of visiting the archaeological remains of Cyprus were fast vanishing.

'Miss Evans must come, too,' Katerina interrupted, as if reading her thoughts. 'You promised to show her Pegeia, remember? You can come on here afterwards.'

Andreas insisted on taking them on a tour of the house. It had a surprising number of rooms, all with plain, whitewashed walls and small windows that would keep out the hot sun of summer and the cold winds of winter. Many of them were clean but empty.

'This house was built for a large

family and their farmhands,' Andreas explained. 'You always had two or three generations living and working alongside each other.'

The wing that formed the L-shape had apparently been built at a time when the family had expanded even beyond the limits of the house.

'This has not been used for many years,' Andreas said regretfully. 'It needs a lot of work done to it now. At one time I thought Katerina could move in when she got married, but I don't think that will happen now.'

He said nothing about the problems with Demetrius and the inheritance, and after they had inspected the house he insisted on toasting his new friends with glasses of fiery Cypriot brandy. By then the light was already showing signs of fading.

'We had better go now,' James said reluctantly, 'or we will never get back to Paphos.' He turned to Katerina. 'Are you on duty this evening? Would you like a lift?'

She thanked him but said she would not be on duty again until the following morning.

'I look forward to seeing you then,' James told her, and Lorna thought she saw the girl blush slightly.

The minor road took them back via Pegeia, but it was too late to explore the place and they carried on to the main coastal road.

'I assume it was Katerina who was talking to you about the Akamas,' Lorna commented at one point.

'Yes. She is a very intelligent young woman who loves the area.'

'But she is afraid of losing her home,' and Lorna told James about the four inheritors. He was obviously disturbed by the threat to the area.

'There are too many tacky estates and holiday camps already!' he said hotly. 'The whole peninsula is supposed to be protected by UNESCO and should be preserved as a national park.'

All in all, Lorna had enjoyed the day, and she told James as much and thanked him warmly when they finally arrived back at the Hotel Persepolis.

'I might go back to help Andreas tomorrow,' he said, 'but I won't offer to take you. Katerina won't be there, and if Andreas and I are busy that would mean you would be on your own or with that nasty little brother for company.'

'Don't worry. I am planning to copy you and be the typical holidaymaker — swimming and sunbathing.'

'But you will come out me again another day, won't you?' He sounded genuinely anxious for her company and Lorna felt flattered as she went up to her room after assuring him that she was very willing to explore Cyprus with him on some other occasion.

True to her word, she lazed around the pool for most of the next day. She saw Katerina at Reception when she went in for lunch.

'Thank you for welcoming two lost tourists to your home yesterday,' she said, and Katerina laughed.

'I should thank you for coming! Andreas and James are obviously soul mates. I haven't seen my brother so happy for ages!'

At this point the assistant manager appeared and Katerina told him about Lorna and James's unintended visit. He was obviously amused.

'You found the house by accident? I have been there, and it took me hours to find it!'

In the late afternoon Lorna took advantage of one of the hotel's facilities and went to the computer room to check on her emails but found there was nothing that could not wait till she returned home. That took ten minutes, but as she had paid for an hour she was idly browsing through various websites when she remembered that James had told her that he had a site.

James Young typed into a search engine soon took her to the site, and she was very impressed. Instead of the rustic furniture which she had half-expected, there were covetable, elegant pieces in beautiful woods. Lorna's eyes widened at the prices. If James was charging so much and still selling his pieces, he must be doing very well indeed. She also found a section which dealt with his sculptures in wood, which he had not mentioned. They were beautiful, abstract shapes. Lorna decided that she would save hard and try to buy one, but that it might take some time. Perhaps, if they stayed friends, she might receive one as a gift.

At dinner Aunt Anne listened to Lorna's account of her day, but obviously found it less than thrilling.

'So you went to a farm and helped Katerina with the vegetables? That sounds nice,' she said dutifully, before launching into an account of her own encounter with an elaborately dressed Greek Orthodox bishop in Paphos.

'That sounds nice,' Lorna said dutifully in her turn.

James was late for dinner, but very happy.

'Andreas and I have practically

finished that balcony,' he told Lorna over coffee. 'And we looked at the wing of the house they don't use. It's neglected, but basically it is not in bad condition. We had some ideas about what it could be used for, providing that Demetrius doesn't get his way and sell the farm. I said I would go back tomorrow. Katerina will be there for most of the day, so will you come with me?'

Lorna decided she could spend a full day at the farm without getting too bored — particularly as James would be there.

6

As James wanted to get an early start, Lorna and he were the first into the dining room for breakfast. He proved to be annoyingly alert and lively so early in the morning, though it took more than one cup of coffee to make Lorna feel human.

They set off through the streets of Paphos, which seemed eerily quiet at this hour of the day. Most of the tourists and those who catered to their needs — the restaurant and bar owners and staff — were still recovering from the exertions of the previous night.

'I like it like this,' James said when she commented on it. 'I know that people come to Paphos for the sun and the nightlife, but at this time of the morning you can see what the town used to be like before so many hotels went up and you can see the really good buildings.' He waved at a church. 'Look at that. It's meant to dominate the area, not be hemmed in by apartment blocks.'

She looked at him curiously.

'Have you been to Cyprus before?' she asked.

'I've only been abroad a couple of times. I went camping in France with my family when I was a teenager, and I had a week in Spain when I was twenty — but I spent all my time on the beach and in bars, so don't ask me what Spain was like!'

'Would you come to Cyprus again?'

He nodded emphatically.

'The history, the landscape, the trees — it has a lot to offer me.'

'And you seem to have a lot to offer Andreas.'

'I'm grateful to him. He's introducing me to the real Cyprus beyond the tourist resorts. Look!'

He was pointing at a yard piled high with logs. On the gate was a sign: *Lemon, olive and carob wood for fires.*

'Fancy being able to sit by a fire smelling of those fruit woods,' James sighed. 'In England you'd just have a notice saying, 'Firewood', and you wouldn't have the slightest idea which trees it had come from.'

When they arrived at the farm, it was clear that Katerina had been up for hours. The neat kitchen smelled of slow-cooking meat and freshly-baked bread and Katerina welcomed them with fresh coffee.

'Drink it before Andreas drags you off,' she instructed James. 'He seems to have decided that you are the answer to his prayers.'

'I'm glad to be able to help,' James protested.

'And I am most grateful to you for helping,' Katerina said with great sincerity, and Lorna saw her gaze at James with something approaching affection.

In fact Andreas did appear soon and had to be persuaded to let James finish his coffee before he took him away.

Katerina looked at Lorna enquiringly.

'How would you like to spend the day?'

'Oh, I don't want to disturb your routine,' Lorna said hastily. 'I'll just help you or wander around.'

Katerina shook her head decisively.

'My day is free. Lunch is cooking already. If you like, we can look round the farm and the surrounding area.'

And that was what they did. There were chickens and a large vegetable plot near the house, but the fields showed that the farm did not rely on one crop. There were olives, glossy banana plants and other trees which were apparently carob trees whose seeds could be used as a substitute for chocolate or for making syrup.

'What is your main crop?' Lorna wanted to know.

'At the moment, bananas.' Katerina looked a little despondent. 'We used to grow vines, but the rainfall grew less, so we grow bananas instead. But now there is often not enough rain for the bananas, so I don't know what we will start growing next.'

'Perhaps Demetrius has a point,' Lorna ventured. 'If it is so difficult to grow profitable crops . . . '

Katerina was shaking her head. 'We can survive as farmers, but once a beautiful place is lost to bricks and concrete it is gone for ever.'

Lorna stayed tactfully silent for a while before broaching a new subject.

'How do you see your future? Are you going to continue to work at the hotel and live here?'

There was a touch of mischief in Katerina's smile.

'I will go on doing that until I marry.'

'And when will that be?' Lorna turned to her with interest. 'Have you met someone you want to marry?'

Katerina's smile grew wider.

'I think so, but I am not sure that he has realised yet that he is going to marry me, so I'm not going to tell you any more about him.'

'Do I know him?'

84

'You have met him,' Katerina said enigmatically, but refused to be drawn any further on the subject.

'Where is Demetrius today?' Lorna asked finally, and Katerina's smile vanished abruptly.

'He is at college — at least, that is where he is supposed to be. I am afraid that sometimes he just goes into town to meet his friends.'

'He will settle down,' Lorna said comfortingly. 'After all, you and Andreas are setting him good examples.'

Katerina was still sad.

'I think the trouble is that he is the youngest and because he is very like our mother, who died when he was only eight years old, my father spoiled him and made excuses for anything he did wrong. As a result, he has had to take very little responsibility for his actions.'

'He will learn, and hopefully the lesson won't be too hard.'

Their wanderings had brought them to a small, one-street village. Some of the houses were closed and shuttered, but villagers waved and called a greeting to Katerina when they saw her.

'There used to be more people living here when I was a child, but as agriculture has declined many families have moved away,' she told Lorna, and then pointed at a miniature church. 'I used to go there every Sunday — I still go sometimes when I am not on duty.'

Lorna peered in the church. Byzantine saints decorated the sanctuary end, and she saw the dull gleam of silver.

'Is it safe to leave the silver in an unlocked church?'

'It is during the day, because the villagers would see any strangers, and the church is locked at night. Anyway, there are only a few plates and a chalice, though I believe they are quite old.'

Someone called Katerina's name and she looked down the street and waved cheerily.

'It's Maria — a friend of mine.'

The girl who joined them was plump and pleasant-looking. She studied Lorna with obvious interest when Katerina introduced them and told her that Lorna was visiting the farm.

'Do you like it? Don't you think Andreas works hard?'

Lorna nodded vigorously.

'He is a very good farmer.'

The girl smiled with satisfaction before turning to her friend to make arrangements to meet some time.

'You can't praise Andreas too much as far as Maria is concerned,' Katerina remarked on their way back to the farm. 'She and Andreas have been sweethearts since they were children.'

'When are they getting married?'

Katerina shook her head sadly.

'How can they get married when Andreas doesn't know if he will be able to support a wife and family?'

Back at the house, Katerina started to prepare for lunch, but Lorna asked if she could wander round the farm by herself for a bit.

'I've brought my camera, and I'd like to take some photos of the flowers.

There are some I've never seen before.'

Away from the house Lorna started looking for unusual plants. The search led her away from the carefully-tended fields into a wooded area and she was snapping happily away when she became aware of an incongruous sound. Someone nearby was snoring loudly. Carefully Lorna crept towards the source of the noise until she peered round a tree trunk into a small glade. There she saw that it was Demetrius, asleep in the sunshine, who was snoring so loudly. His motorbike was beside him, and clasped to his chest was a half-empty bottle of wine. So Katerina's fears had been true. Instead of studying so that he could help his family, he was avoiding college and idling his day away.

Lorna moved quietly back into the woods and then returned to the farmhouse. On the way she brooded on what she should do about her discovery, but decided not to tell Katerina or Andreas what she had seen. She did not know them well enough to interfere in their family affairs. However, she resolved that if she ever got the opportunity she would have a strong word with Demetrius himself.

Everybody ate the lamb stew with relish and then relaxed round the table with fruit grown on the farm and a glass of wine. Andreas and James were very satisfied with the progress they had made.

'I keep asking this man what I can give him in return for his help.' Andreas sighed. 'All he says is that he is enjoying himself and doesn't want anything.'

'Not quite true,' James interrupted. 'I did say I would be grateful for some bits of olive wood.'

'How could you get those back to England?' Katerina laughed.

James smiled sheepishly, running his fingers through his untidy hair.

'I could manage some small pieces — just interesting shapes — in my luggage if I abandoned a few shoes and things.' He looked hopefully at Lorna. 'Will you have any space when we go back, Lorna?'

She shook her head ruefully.

'If I have any space to spare, I am afraid Aunt Anne will want to fill it. She's been doing quite a lot of shopping.'

Andreas put a comforting hand on James's shoulder.

'Tell me which pieces you want, and I will keep them till you come again. Then you can work on them here.'

'That might not be for years!' James said mournfully, but Andreas shook his head.

'No, we are friends now and you will come back to see us and you will stay here, in this house.'

Katerina was smiling and nodding and Lorna felt a pang of jealousy. James was welcome, but her presence was only tolerated because she had come with him. She would not be welcomed as a guest for her own sake. But now Andreas was smiling at her as well.

'Lorna, if it hadn't been for your

map-reading I would never have met James. I hope to see you again, too.'

Lorna blushed with pleasure and then blushed again as Katerina said mischievously, 'Perhaps Lorna will marry one of the islanders — a farmer, perhaps — and stay here for ever.'

'An excellent idea! Let's drink to that!' Andreas laughed, and Lorna thought for a fleeting moment how attractive he looked when his eyes crinkled with laughter.

They took Katerina with them back to the hotel that afternoon. She had changed into her trim uniform and Lorna noticed James eyeing her appreciatively. After she had thanked them and disappeared into the building, Lorna told James about her sighting of Demetrius. He frowned and muttered a few words under his breath.

'Andreas was telling me about the problems they have had with that boy. He is worried about so-called friends who are having a bad effect on him.'

'Do you think I did right not to tell them?'

He agreed emphatically.

'Remember, we are only here for a few days. We mustn't interfere and cause trouble and then leave them to sort it out. Let's forget Demetrius.'

But that was not possible. After dinner, sitting having coffee with her aunt, Lorna glanced across at the reception desk and saw that Demetrius was standing there, talking to Katerina. Near him a tall young man in a sharply-cut suit was leaning against the desk, eyeing the guests with a half-concealed sneer. Demetrius appeared to be arguing with Katerina, who finally gave a despairing shrug, disappeared into the office for a moment, and returned with something which she handed to Demetrius. He pushed it into his pocket and gave an abrupt nod. His friend stood up languidly and the two made for the front door.

Lorna's gaze followed them and then she looked up and realized that Ben was standing beside her, also frowning at the two young men as they disappeared through the door.

'I know that one of them is Katerina's brother. Do you know who the other one is?' Lorna asked Ben.

He nodded.

'He's called Leonidas, and he is the son of a wealthy property developer. He seems to do nothing but spend his father's money, and Demetrius is a fool if he is trying to keep up with him. He can't afford it.'

'I think I saw Katerina give Demetrius some money just now,' Lorna said unhappily, and Ben's lips tightened.

'It's time that lad realised how much he owes to his sister and brother. He should be trying to earn some money to help them instead of wasting Katerina's wages on the Paphos night life.'

Aunt Anne was growing curious about Lorna's daytime activities.

'You say it is quite a large farmhouse, and just the two brothers and Katerina live there?'

'Yes, but I don't know how long that will go on for. I think Demetrius will leave as soon as he can, and Andreas is obviously finding it difficult to make the farm pay its way nowadays.'

'I think I'd like to see this place,' her aunt remarked. 'Do you think your James could fit me in his vehicle for a day?'

'I'm sure he could,' Lorna responded a little reluctantly as she tried to imagine Aunt Anne and Andreas together. Then she added hastily, 'But he's not *my* James. It's just that we have been thrown together and we get on quite well.'

Aunt Anne made no comment, but Lorna saw a small, smug smile appear briefly, which irritated her considerably.

*   *   *

James and Lorna set out together again the following day, but this time they were travelling by coach in the company of a score of other tourists who wanted to visit the Troodos Mountains. It was a pleasure to leave behind the sea and the tourist resorts and drive up through thick forests where villages clung to the hillsides and ancient monasteries reminded them of Cyprus's long history. James, however, seemed rather abstracted, and he was clearly less than fascinated by the tour guide's information.

'Is anything the matter?' Lorna asked him quietly when she spoke to him and he did not seem to hear her at first.

'Not with me. I keep thinking about Andreas. Apparently the four brothers and sisters are having a meeting with the lawyers tomorrow morning and he's worried about the outcome.'

'Will you see him tomorrow?'

'I hope to go over in the afternoon.'

'Well, I hope you'll be able to tell me that he has good news.'

He looked at her in sudden alarm.

'Won't you be coming with me? I took it for granted that you would.'

Lorna was conscious of a warm glow, but then he went on. 'I think Katerina gets a bit lonely there and she will be glad of your company.'

So he wanted her to go for Katerina's sake!

'I'll have to see if my aunt has anything planned for us,' she said stiffly.

'Please come if you can. Andreas likes you. He disapproves of most tourists, but he thinks you are sensible and intelligent.' James gave a sudden grin. 'He likes your hair, as well.'

Lorna's iciness started to thaw. Anyway, she wanted to know whether the fate of the farm had been decided.

'I'll try to come,' she promised.

The coach returned to the hotel in plenty of time for the tourists to relax, change, and come downstairs for a pre-dinner drink before enjoying the hotel's excellent food. Lorna was finding it hard to reconcile the contrasting faces of Cyprus — the comfortable hotels, the isolated farms and small villages, the beaches and the soaring mountains. And she hadn't really started on the ancient sites dotted through the island! She would definitely return.

During the next day's journey to Katerina's home, both Lorna and James were apprehensive, wondering what they would find there. Suppose she and her brother had been told that they would have to sell the farm? But when they arrived they found there had still been no clear-cut decision. Agnes, the elder sister, had decided that she would like to have her share of the inheritance in cash, but had indicated that she would prefer to sell to Andreas rather than a developer.

'But what good is that?' Andreas demanded. 'She has given me two months to find the money to buy her out, but she knows I can't raise that amount. The burden of debt would be too great.' He glanced round. 'At least Demetrius is staying with her tonight, otherwise we would probably be quarrelling now.'

'So the two of you want to keep the farm and the other two want to sell — deadlock!' James commented. He slapped Andreas on the back. 'Well, you can't do anything about it now, so come and work some of your black mood off with some hard labour.'

'And what shall we do to cheer ourselves up?' Katerina asked as the two girls wandered out into the courtyard. Lorna noticed Katerina's moped propped against the wall. She went over and fingered the controls.

'I used to have one of these,' she said, 'but only for a short time. There is too much traffic in England and I was scared of every car that came near me.'

'I don't have that problem round here,' Katerina replied. 'It is very handy when I have to get to the hotel by myself.' She turned to Lorna. 'Do you remember how to ride it . . . ?'

Five minutes later, the two girls were jolting along the path on the moped, Lorna clutching Katerina's waist, both giggling at each bump.

'It's like a fairground ride,' gasped Lorna.

Katerina's laughter stopped suddenly.

'Bother! I've just noticed that I am nearly out of petrol! Andreas will have to load it on his van and take it to the petrol station in the next village. I'm always forgetting to fill it up!'

7

Because Lorna and James had not arrived till the afternoon, they stayed later than usual. Andreas and James stopped work as the light began to fade and Katerina was pouring wine for them all when the telephone rang. Andreas picked it up and after the caller's first few words he started barking urgent questions. Katerina stood still, her eyes fixed on him, till he slammed the telephone down and turned to the three of them, his face twisted with anxiety.

'That was a neighbour of Agnes, our sister. There has been an accident. Agnes and her husband are in hospital in Nicosia and the neighbour's wife is looking after the children. I must go and see what has happened. Katerina, can I bring the children back here?'

'Of course!' his sister said unhesitatingly. 'Did the neighbour tell you what had happened?'

'No, just that I should come at once, so it must be bad.'

'Go this minute,' Katerina said, pushing him towards the door. 'Call me as soon as you have news, and I'll get beds ready for the children.' She stopped. 'What about Demetrius? He was supposed to be staying with Agnes tonight.'

'The man didn't say anything about him. I'll find out when I get there.'

Soon Lorna and Katerina were busy airing bedding and trying to decide what the children would feel like eating, but just as they had agreed on some home-made soup, the telephone rang again.

'That can't be Andreas — he hasn't been gone long enough,' Katerina said, picking it up. Whoever was calling, Katerina was not happy when the call ended, and she explained why to Lorna and James.

'That was the hotel. They want me to go in at once. Apparently two of the reception staff have been taken ill. But I can't go! I've got to get things ready for the children and wait for them and Andreas. But the hotel may hold it against me if I don't go in and I need the job.'

'Leave things to me,' Lorna said firmly. 'I can make up the beds and heat the soup.'

'Are you sure?'

'I can cope.'

Katerina's face fell suddenly.

'But I can't get to the hotel. I haven't got enough petrol in my moped, remember?'

Now it was James's turn to help.

'I can take you to the hotel while Lorna stays here and waits for Andreas to call. Then I'll come back and stay here with her until he arrives, and afterwards we can both go back to the hotel.'

Katerina protested weakly, but was overruled. With her moped on the back of the jeep, she and James drove off with Lorna waving good-bye. Then Lorna went slowly back into the farmhouse and closed the door. It was growing dark and suddenly she felt very alone and isolated in this unfamiliar land.

She busied herself preparing beds for the children and other little tasks. Afterwards she decided she had earned a glass of wine and was sitting by the light of the fire drinking it when she thought she heard the sound of an engine. Surely James hadn't got back so quickly? But when she opened the door there was silence and nothing to be seen. A little later there was a sudden commotion in the hen house. Lorna's heart jumped, but she told herself it was probably a fox or some other would-be predator. Did they have foxes in Cyprus? The noise subsided, but then the telephone rang, almost startling her into dropping her glass.

It was Andreas. He asked for Katerina, but Lorna explained that she was at the farm by herself and told him why.

'I don't know what's happening,' Andreas said angrily. 'I think someone is playing a cruel trick. Halfway to Nicosia I stopped and used my mobile to call the hospital, and I was told that my sister and brother-in-law were not there, and had not been there for any reason today. So then I called Agnes' house, and she answered. She and her husband are safe and well and the two children are with them. Demetrius told her he was going to see a friend, so I don't know where he is. I am coming back to the farm immediately.'

Lorna realised she was gripping the telephone as tightly as she could. 'How long will you be, Andreas? I must admit I'm not very happy here on my own. I don't know which farm noises are normal noises and which aren't.'

'I'll be back as soon as possible.'

Lorna shakily decided she needed another glass of wine. Who could have telephoned, and why? It occurred to her that because of the coincidence of Katerina being summoned back to the hotel, the hoax telephone call would have meant that if she and James had not chanced to be visiting the farm it would now have been left empty and deserted. Had someone wanted that? If that were so, what was supposed to be happening at the farm now?

She sat huddled in her chair, listening as hard as she could, unconsciously holding her breath. She could hear nothing. There was utter silence. She took a deep breath and relaxed, scolding herself for being such an urban coward.

Then, suddenly, she heard a roar and the window was filled with brilliant, burning light. Lorna dashed to the door and threw it open, terrified that she was going to be trapped in a burning building. Once outside she saw that a wooden shed which stood next to the house was blazing fiercely. Katerina had told her the shed held animal feed which Lorna knew would burn, but not as fiercely as this. She became aware of a strong smell of petrol. Somebody had doused the shed with petrol and set it alight, and soon the flames would spread to the house!

What could she do? She dashed back into the house and lifted the telephone receiver, but the line was dead, either cut or destroyed by the fire.

Smoke was rolling through the door and she ran out again and stood in the courtyard, coughing as the acrid smoke filled her lungs. Lorna stepped back, away from the intense heat of the flames, and then screamed involuntarily as she felt herself collide with solid flesh.

She turned, but now the smoke was filling her eyes with tears and all she could see was a dark figure lunging towards her. Terrified, she ran out of the courtyard towards the fields and woods, stumbling over the rough ground until she had found shelter in the trees where she ran on until she found herself in pitch darkness and stopped, cowering in the shelter of a large tree.

There was no sound of pursuit and she sank to the ground, sobbing. The sky was overcast that night and she could see nothing and had lost all sense of direction. The nearest place where she could find help was the small village but she had no idea where it was.

She would have to wait till morning to find out which direction she should go in. Meanwhile, because she had run away like a coward, Andreas and Katerina were losing their home. Lorna wept, her head on her knees.

She did not know how long she had been crouched there when she became aware of a voice in the distance. Lifting her head, she realised that someone was calling her name. She sprang up, uncertain where the sound was coming from, and managed to waver 'Help!' The voice stopped, and then restarted more urgently.

'Lorna! Where are you?'

'Help me! I'm here!'

There seemed to be a long pause, and then Lorna saw the light of a torch among the trees. She ran towards it, fell over a tree root, got up and started running again, and found herself held tightly in James's arms. She was shivering and crying uncontrollably and he held her, murmuring comforting words, till she had regained some control and could speak.

'The farmhouse! Someone was trying to burn it down!'

'It's all right,' James told her. 'Andreas and I got back just in the nick of time. Some of woodwork had started to smoulder, but Andreas produced a hose and we managed to save the house. Now, can you walk back to the farm or have I got to try to carry you?'

Lorna produced a sound between a laugh and a snort.

'Let me hold your arm and I think I can make it.'

And they did make it, though James's arm was round her and he was virtually supporting her by the time they reached the courtyard where Katerina was waiting. The two of them took her into the house and sat her in a chair where she gratefully closed her eyes. A second later, they were open again and she was trying to stand up.

'Someone was here! I bumped into him. He may still be here!'

James shook his head.

'Andreas got here a few minutes before me and he said he heard a car engine driving away along the road just before he turned into the approach to the farm. That must have been the arsonist making his escape.'

Lorna was frowning at Katerina, puzzled by her presence.

'I thought you were wanted at the hotel.'

'Another false telephone call, so James and I drove back as fast as we could to see what was going on.'

Now Andreas appeared and gratefully took the cup of coffee which Katerina offered him. Lorna realised that all three had smoke-stained clothes and faces blackened by soot.

'The fire is out,' Andreas told them. 'We've lost the animal feed and the shed, but nothing else has been damaged beyond repair.' He wiped a tired hand across his eyes. 'If I hadn't got back when I did — and if James hadn't appeared so soon after me — the house would have burned to the ground.'

'Who could have done such a thing?' Lorna demanded, but Andreas only answered with a shrug.

'There are people who just like to see things burn. Our main worry was what had happened to you. Once we'd dealt with the fire we started looking for you, and when we couldn't find you James guessed you might have run for the woods and went looking for you.'

Lorna felt as if it were the middle of the night, but was surprised to be told that it was only about ten o'clock.

'Aunt Anne will be wondering what on earth has happened to me,' she exclaimed, but Katerina shook her head.

'I saw your aunt when I went into the

hotel and explained what had happened. I told her that you would be back late, and that you might in fact stay here for the night. Would you like to do that?'

Lorna was tempted. The idea of having to move, to endure a journey back to the hotel, was daunting. It would be so much easier to stay here, but she saw James shake his head slightly.

He was right, of course. Andreas and Katerina would have to deal with the after effects of the fire, even though they were already completely exhausted. They did not need a helpless visitor. Lorna forced herself to her feet.

'It is a very kind offer, and I thank you, but I'd better get back to the hotel and my aunt.'

'I'll get you a jacket to keep you warm.'

Katerina went in search of a suitable garment. Andreas had gone outside to check on the chickens, so Lorna and James were briefly left alone. Lorna took a few steps to put her cup on the table and almost fell over a black bundle lying in the shadow of her chair.

'What's that?' James asked.

It was heavy and clinked when Lorna picked it up. Something was rolled in a length of cloth and when she folded it back the dull gleam of silver was revealed. Suddenly she recognised what she was holding.

'James! These are the silver dishes and the chalice from the little church I told you about — the one in the village! Whoever set light to the hut must have stolen them!'

James's face set hard as he took the bundle from her to inspect the objects. Then, as they heard Katerina coming back, he rapidly wrapped the cloth round them and put his finger to his lips as a sign that Lorna should keep quiet about their find. She was puzzled, but obeyed.

A few minutes later, James helped her into the jeep, with the bundle under one arm, and they set off on their return journey, but as soon as they were out of sight and sound of the farm,

James steered the jeep to the side of the road and switched off the engine.

'We have a problem,' he said grimly, staring straight ahead into the moonlit night. 'Who is always in need of more money and wants to see the farm sold to developers?'

'Demetrius, of course,' Lorna answered, and then her eyes widened. 'Do you think he robbed the church and then tried to set fire to the farm?'

'I don't want to think that, but I am afraid it is possible. That is why I stopped you telling Katerina about the church silver. He had left Agnes's house, so we don't know where he has been tonight. A brother who tries to burn the house down is bad enough, but if it turns out that he has robbed a church as well that would break her heart.'

Lorna noticed that it was Katerina he was thinking of — Andreas was not mentioned — but that was not important. Her dominating emotion was fury at the thought that a selfish youth could destroy the world of Andreas and Katerina, and put an end to Maria's hopes as well.

'So what do we do?'

'Well, first of all, we return the silver to its rightful place,' and he started the engine again.

It was only a few minutes to the village, and in spite of the lateness of the hour there was a light in the church. James parked the jeep and picked up the bundle, Lorna stiffly got out of her seat, and together they approached the church and hesitantly opened the door. Inside, as its old hinges creaked protestingly, a tall, grey-bearded man in shirt sleeves and black trousers sprang round to face them, a shotgun in his hands. James raised a hand in urgent protest.

'Stop! We don't mean any harm.'

The man lowered the shotgun slightly so it was no longer pointing directly at them, but his expression was still threatening.

'This is no hour for tourists to come

sightseeing. Why are you here?'

'It isn't normal for anyone to be guarding a church with a shotgun, either. We came to return these.'

He held out the bundle, turning back the cloth to show what it held. The man set his gun aside and took the bundle eagerly, examining its contents carefully before looking up at them.

'I found the church door had been forced, and the silver stolen. What do you know about it?'

'Nothing,' James said firmly, 'except we found this bundle by chance, recognised its contents and knew we had to return them.'

Suddenly the man was smiling.

'Then I am most grateful on behalf of the village.' The frown returned as he inspected the silver again. 'But the lid of the chalice is missing.'

Lorna groaned, but James looked the man in the eye steadily.

'You have my word that I will do my best to find the chalice lid and return it to you.'

The two men regarded each other in silence, and then the Cypriot nodded.

'I believe you, and I hope to see you soon. Thank you again for bringing the silver back to its church.'

Then it was back to the jeep. Exhausted after all the drama, Lorna was soon nodding off to sleep and it came as something of a shock when James stopped again and announced that they had arrived back at the Hotel Persepolis. Lorna stared gratefully up at its familiar elegant facade.

Perhaps now she could return to her normal life. But first she and James, both tired, their clothes showing the effects of smoke and their passage through the woods, had to reach their rooms while trying not to excite the curiosity of the few guests who were still up. Quietly they slipped along the wall to the bank of lifts.

'I'll see you to your room,' James murmured.

'There's no need. I can manage.'

James gave a wry grin.

'I'm afraid you don't look as if you can. I don't want you found unconscious in the corridor.'

She allowed him to take her up to her floor and then to her door. In fact she was quite glad of his hand supporting her elbow. She fumbled for her plastic room key, managed to fit it into the slot, and James reached across and turned the handle, opening the door.

'I think I can safely say goodnight now,' he said softly, but at that moment the door opposite was flung open and Aunt Anne stood there wrapped in a scarlet dressing-gown.

'So you are back at last, Lorna!' She blinked and took in the scene. 'Mr Young, what are doing with my niece?' Another look, and she had registered the state they were in and her voice rose. 'What on earth have you two been up to?'

She strode across the corridor and seized Lorna, while James tried to hush her.

'We don't want to wake the hotel up!

Lorna is all right. She just needs a bath, and you might get her something to eat from room service.' He turned to Lorna. 'I'll see you in the morning.'

And then he fled before Aunt Anne could interrogate him. Left alone with Lorna, her aunt guided her into her room, where she promptly collapsed on the bed. Soon she could hear the bath running and her aunt's concerned face loomed over her.

'Get out of those clothes. What do you want to drink and are you hungry?'

'I'm starving,' Lorna realised, 'and I'd love a pot of tea.'

'Get in the bath and I'll see what I can do.'

Lorna undressed with clumsy fingers and then sank gratefully into the warm bath. She relaxed and closed her eyes, feeling sleep very near.

'You can wash your hair in the morning.' It was her aunt, bearing a tray. 'Now get out and eat this.'

Lorna obeyed, and, wrapped in her towelling dressing-gown, she gratefully ate the cheese omelette and bread which her aunt had ordered, and then drained two cups of tea while her aunt waited patiently. When she put her cup down her aunt picked it up, put it on the tray, and, as quietly as possible, she opened the door and placed the tray in the corridor outside.

'Now you can tell me what has been happening . . . ' she began, and then stopped. Lorna was fast asleep on the bed. Her aunt gazed at her, shrugged resignedly, pulled the covers over her niece, turned out the light, and returned to her own room.

8

Lorna woke late the following morning after a night of confused dreams. She lay quietly for a while, letting yesterday's memories gradually come back, and then realised that she was hungry and would therefore have to get up. Her aunt's door was shut as she made her way down to the restaurant, arriving just in time for a quick breakfast. There was still no sign of her aunt or of James, and Lorna decided that she did not have the energy to go looking for either of them. Instead she went out into the gardens, found an empty sun lounger in a quiet shady spot, sank down and closed her eyes. One minute later, another sun lounger was pulled alongside her and her aunt's voice said firmly, 'And now you can tell me everything.'

Lorna groaned and opened her eyes resentfully.

'We were at a farm and one of the sheds caught fire, that's all.'

Aunt Anne was steely-eyed.

'I got hold of your James Young earlier. He told me part of the story, and then nearly fell asleep in front of me. When I prodded him, he said you would tell me the rest.'

There was no escape. Lorna tried to give a brief account of the past few days, but Aunt Anne demanded more details until, resignedly, Lorna went back to her first drive with James and told her everything that had happened since. When she had finished, her aunt sat silent for a while.

'Poor Katerina,' she said at last, shaking her head. 'And poor Andreas.'

'It's bad enough having the house nearly burned down,' Lorna said unhappily, 'but it will break their hearts if it turns out that Demetrius was responsible.'

Her aunt patted Lorna's knee a little awkwardly.

'But if he was staying a friend in

Nicosia he couldn't have been the arsonist,' she pointed out.

This comforted Lorna a little, and she could smile happily when James appeared bearing a tray with three cups of coffee balanced carefully on it. They accepted the drinks gratefully.

'We must be wrong about Demetrius,' Lorna said eagerly. 'If he was in Nicosia he couldn't have been at the farm.'

James shook his head grimly.

'I called Andreas this morning. He said that there was no point in us going over there, as he and Katerina are still trying to clean things up. I asked him if Demetrius knew what had happened to the farm.' He paused. 'Andreas said he had telephoned Agnes's house this morning and she told him that Demetrius had changed his mind about staying there and had left her some time in the afternoon, saying he was going to see a friend in Limassol, not Nicosia. He would have had time to reach the farm — and the church.'

The three of them sat in gloomy silence, until Aunt Anne sat up briskly.

'Well, it's not your problem. There is nothing you can do.'

James glanced at her.

'Except that I promised to return some missing silver to the church.'

'That was rash of you,' Aunt Anne pronounced. 'Now, Katerina and Andreas don't want you, so why don't you take it easy and enjoy the holiday you expected to have? Sunbathe, go for a swim, walk along the beach like ordinary tourists!'

In fact there was little else they could do. Gradually the tension slackened, and by lunchtime they had recovered enough to consider taking a drive along the coast road to some Roman ruins in the afternoon. After their meal, Lorna and James were sitting in the reception area studying a guide book and deciding exactly where to go, when James suddenly grasped Lorna's arm, his fingers digging deeply into her flesh. She gave an involuntary yelp and turned to him indignantly, but he was staring across at the reception desk.

'Look!' he hissed.

Demetrius was standing by the desk, apparently arguing with the under-manager who usually worked with Katerina. The manager was shaking his head in response to angry questions.

James stood up and made for the desk with Lorna close behind him.

'Hello, Demetrius! What's the problem?'

Demetrius swung round at the interruption, looked at them blankly, frowned, and then finally recognised them.

'I want to speak to Katerina,' he demanded. 'I know that she is supposed to be on duty today, but this man says she isn't here.'

The under-manager intervened. 'Katerina has problems at home. I told her she could take the day off.'

James stared at Demetrius for some long seconds.

'Do you know any reason why she shouldn't be here?'

'No. There were no problems when I saw her yesterday morning.'

James put a hand on Demetrius's arm.

'Come with us. There are things you should know — if you don't know already.'

He steered the young man out into the gardens, to a quiet shady corner where the three of them sat down.

'Someone tried to burn your farm down yesterday evening,' James said without preamble.

Demetrius blanched and half-rose.

'What? Are Katerina and Andreas safe? Who did it?'

He saw how Lorna and James were looking at him accusingly and shook his head violently.

'You said, 'If you don't know already'! No! You think I already knew about it, you think I did it!'

'If the farmhouse had burned down, Andreas and Katerina would have had no option left but to sell the land. You want that. You want your inheritance in cash so that you can spend it on yourself.'

'But I would never have done anything criminal like that! Are they safe?'

James nodded.

'They are both safe and the damage to the house was minimal.'

Demetrius drew in a sobbing breath of relief. The cynical, time-wasting pseudo-sophisticate had gone. Now they were looking at a young man who seemed genuinely appalled at what had been done to his home and family.

'I can prove I was nowhere near the farm,' he said unsteadily. 'I stayed with a friend and his family in Limassol. They can bear witness that I was there from late afternoon till this morning. You must believe me.'

His sincerity was obvious and Lorna and James glanced at each other, their suspicion of his guilt fading fast.

'Then who else could it have been?' Lorna said. 'Who else would benefit? Could it have been someone who just saw the chance to amuse himself by committing arson?'

'Very unlikely,' James said heavily. 'It was a pretty elaborate plot to get Katerina and Andreas away from the farm. Somebody must have known about their sister and where Katerina worked. And remember the church silver. An arsonist who is also a thief? He would have broken into the farm to see what was worth stealing before he tried to set fire to it.'

Demetrius was looking at him in bewilderment.

'The church silver? What are you talking about?'

Lorna explained to him how they had stumbled upon the bundle of stolen silver and returned it. 'everything but the chalice lid,' James reminded her.

'And we told that man we would find the lid. What chance have we got of doing that?' She sighed, then looked at Demetrius with astonishment as the young man sat rigidly upright in his seat, two vivid spots of colour glaring in his cheeks. His gaze seemed fixed on infinity and his fists were white-knuckled.

'Demetrius! What's the matter?'

Instead of replying, the young Cypriot leapt up, overturning his chair which fell against James's and knocked him to the ground. He ran for the hotel. James picked himself up and he and Lorna ran after Demetrius, whom they saw disappearing through the front door.

By the time they had got through the door, a taxi with Demetrius in it was already speeding out of the drive. They gazed after it in amazement, but there was nothing they could do except return to the gardens and speculate on what Demetrius intended to do.

'He's convinced me that he had nothing to do with the fire,' Lorna said unhappily.

'I felt the same. But where did he have to go in such a hurry, and why didn't he want us to know?'

'Perhaps he wants to get back to the farm and find out if Katerina and

Andreas are really all right,' she guessed.

'If that is so, I will find out tomorrow because I intend to drive over there, whether Katerina and Andreas want us to or not.'

Lorna looked at him with determination.

'In that case, I'm coming with you.'

He grinned.

'I rather took that for granted, Lorna.' He stretched out his long legs and sighed. 'Now, we've still got an afternoon to fill, so are we going off to see these ruins or not?'

'We'd better. Apparently nobody will believe we've been to Cyprus if we haven't got dozens of photographs of this site.'

'Then let us go and do our cultural duty . . . '

*   *   *

In fact, they enjoyed the ruins immensely, only regretting that they would not be able to attend a concert in the amphitheatre with its dramatic back-drop of the sea.

But back at the hotel, Aunt Anne was waiting.

'I understand Katerina's brother appeared earlier and then left in a hurry,' she said smoothly. 'Now you can tell me the rest.'

They told her what had happened, and that they intended to go to the farm the next day.

'Then I'll come with you,' she said firmly.

'It's only a farm, and it is in a mess at the moment. I'm not sure they will welcome us, and as for any other unexpected visitors . . . ' James's voice tailed away as Aunt Anne raised an eyebrow and looked at him icily.

'What time are we leaving?' she asked crisply, and his resistance crumbled.

'I thought we could set off about nine.'

'Lorna and I will be ready.'

So, of course, they were ready. In fact they were standing by the reception desk at ten minutes to nine, and Aunt Anne was already beginning to fidget.

'James said nine o'clock,' Lorna reminded her patiently.

'That means nine o'clock at the latest,' her aunt said. 'I want to see how Katerina is coping.'

There was a polite cough from the under-manager who seemed to be on almost permanent duty.

'Excuse me, but are you going to see the Katerina who works here?'

'Yes. You know there has been trouble at her farm?'

The tall young man nodded gravely.

'I have given her permission to take a few days' leave. However, when you see her I shall be grateful if you will tell her that Alex sends his regards and hopes that her problems will soon be solved.'

'Of course I will,' Lorna said warmly, and was rewarded with a smile which transformed the manager's normally serious face.

'That is if we ever get there,' Aunt Anne said waspishly, but at that moment James appeared and swept them out to the jeep. Aunt Anne spent the first ten minutes of the journey complaining how uncomfortable the vehicle was, but then subsided into silence.

Apart from a burnt patch where the shed had once stood, the farm looked normal enough. Katerina and Andreas greeted them warmly, managing to conceal any surprise they felt at the sight of Aunt Anne. They looked tired, as if they had been working very hard.

'Maria has helped us,' Katerina told Lorna quietly. 'She was here for hours yesterday scrubbing floors. But replacing the shed and repairing what has been damaged will cost money, and that means any hope of marriage to Andreas gets fainter and fainter. I think her family may soon tell her that she must forget him and look for another husband.'

After coffee, Andreas took James away to inspect some repair task he thought the two of them could tackle, leaving the women to enjoy a second cup. Katerina chatted happily enough, but Lorna thought her cheerfulness seemed forced. However, she brightened and managed a mischievous smile when Lorna gave her Alex's message.

'He has been very kind and understanding,' she said primly, but Lorna could see her eyes sparkle and wondered whether Katerina's colleague at the hotel was rival to James for Katerina's affections.

The two girls conducted Aunt Anne round the farmyard and then round the house, where some of the rooms still smelled of smoke. The older woman inspected everything minutely.

'What about that bit?' she asked when they had finished, indicating the empty wing.

Katerina shrugged.

'There is nothing to see there. It has been empty for years.'

'Nevertheless I would like to look round it. Do you mind if I go by myself?'

With permission from Katerina granted, she took herself off and Lorna seized the chance to get more information from her friend.

'What has Demetrius been doing?' she asked, and Katerina's shoulders sagged.

'We haven't seen or heard of him since Nicosia,' she said sadly. 'We have telephoned one or two people but nobody seems to know where he is. Andreas is going to drive into Limassol and look for him tomorrow if we don't hear anything.'

Lorna hesitated, but then decided that Katerina was entitled to know about the appearance of Demetrius at the hotel.

'He seemed very upset when I told him about the fire,' she added at the end of her account, and then said, very emphatically, 'It was obvious that he knew nothing about it.'

Katerina gave a deep sigh.

'That takes a weight off my heart, though I would like to know where he is now. Although we haven't discussed it, I suspect that both Andreas and I were afraid that Demetrius was involved, though I hoped that deep down he cares too much for both of us to do anything so dreadful.' Then she grew sad again. 'But we are wondering whether it is worth trying to carry on. What is the use of working so hard and for so little reward if someone can come along and casually destroy everything?'

Lorna hugged her.

'It was a one-off, Katerina. It won't happen again and no real harm was done.'

But Katerina was crying openly now.

'I keep telling myself that, but it's no good. Everything has changed. I used to feel so safe here in my home, but now I keep feeling that there is some unknown menace threatening us. I'm afraid!'

Lorna tried to comfort her, with some success, and by the time Aunt Anne returned, Katerina had dried her eyes but obviously wanted some time to herself because she suggested that Lorna should take her aunt for a walk round the farm and show her the wild flowers. Fortunately Aunt Anne seemed ready to fall in with this suggestion and the two of them set off on the tour. Lorna dutifully pointed out the rarities she had noticed, but Aunt Anne had never shown any great interest in wild flowers and seemed to be taking very little notice of her niece now. Suddenly she stopped in her tracks and shook her head.

'It's no good, you know.'

Taken aback, Lorna murmured an apology.

'I thought you might like to see some of the plants . . . '

Her aunt gave her an impatient look.

'I can't tell one flower from another and you know it! No, I'm talking about this farm. It's not big enough or fertile enough to survive as it is. Andreas and Katerina might manage to struggle on for a few more years, but eventually they would have to admit defeat. Ben and I have been discussing how Cyprus is altering. The climate is changing and that means the crops are changing, and small independent farmers are finding it harder and harder to make a living.'

'Then what are they doing to survive?'

'Some of them are forming co-operatives and that helps them compete with the bigger farms, but is doesn't sound as though Andreas and Katerina have any neighbours they could join up with. A lot of them are just giving up and selling their land to bigger farmers or to developers.'

'Selling the farm would break their hearts!'

'I know that, but do you want them to wait until they are deep in debt because they have borrowed to try and keep going? Then they would have to sell to pay off what they owed, and would probably end up with nothing.'

Aunt and niece returned to the farm in mutual gloom, which was dissipated by the spectacle of Andreas and James staggering into the courtyard laden with misshapen pieces of tree root.

'Are those for firewood?' Aunt Anne enquired and was rewarded with a horrified glare from James.

'These are beautiful pieces of olive wood, things to be cherished,' he reproved her, lovingly stroking one convoluted lump. 'Andreas has some basic wood-working tools, and I am going to start work on this tomorrow.'

'James says I could sell them at the Persepolis,' Katerina added. 'He says that people will pay good prices for them and the money will help replace the shed.'

'And how many can you do before you go back to England?' Aunt Anne asked with acid sweetness.

James's turned red, but Katerina rushed to his defence.

'We shall be grateful for even one or two.' She turned to James. 'How can we thank you for your help?'

Lorna thought cynically that James's expression as he looked at Katerina answered that question. It seemed clear to her that he was very attracted to the beautiful Cypriot girl. Perhaps he would move to Cyprus to be with her. After all, there would always be plenty of olive wood for him to work on. Why didn't she feel pleased at the possibility of a happy ending for the pair?

Aunt Anne was also watching.

'James is a lot more interesting than I thought at first,' she murmured to Lorna a few minutes later when the two men were out of hearing. 'He's an artist, but he's also a hands-on practical man who can mend a fence as well as creating something desirable from what others would regard as rubbish to be burned.'

'And Katerina?'

'Oh, whoever marries Katerina will be a lucky man. She will make a very good wife.'

'And me? Do you think anyone will ever say that about me?'

Aunt Anne gave Lorna a scathing look.

'Sometimes you are surprisingly stupid, Lorna. Stop under-rating yourself. After all, in some ways you are very like me.'

Lorna wondered if that was meant to cheer her up.

9

The sun would soon be declining in the west and it would be time to drive back to the hotel. Aunt Anne glanced at her watch and looked at Lorna. 'Will you please find James and tell him I want to be back at the hotel in time to have a shower before dinner?'

Lorna rose obediently from her chair in the courtyard where the three women had been sitting and chatting and started to walk towards the noises of hammering and sawing, but she had to leap back as a large car swept round the corner into the courtyard and braked abruptly. It was a sleek, black limousine with darkened windows. After a few seconds, as the women were staring in amazement at this intruder, the driver's door opened and a man stepped out and stood, hands on hips, surveying his surroundings. He was short, dressed in a smart black suit which did little to disguise his stout figure. His thick dark hair stood up like a brush over his skull and the pouches under his dark eyes showed he was well into middle age.

Summoned by the sound of the engine, Andreas and James had reappeared and the newcomer swung to face them. He frowned at James, visibly dismissed him, and turned to Andreas.

'Andreas Mallias?' he asked.

Andreas nodded, eying the citified newcomer suspiciously.

'And you are . . . ?'

'I am Paul Mourikis.'

Andreas gave an angry exclamation.

'I have heard of you, Mr Mourikis. I know you are a developer but I have made it clear that I am not interested in any offer people like you may wish to make me. Now, please get off my property!'

Mr Mourikis raised his eyebrows. Obviously, people were not usually so unwelcoming.

'Don't jump to conclusions, Mallias. I haven't come to make you an offer but to return some property to you.' He stepped up to the rear door of his limousine and threw it open dramatically. 'I bring you your brother!'

Demetrius almost tumbled out onto the courtyard but managed to retain his footing and stood up, pulling his clothing into order. Katerina cried his name and he turned towards her, revealing to everyone a battered, bruised face. Andreas tightened his grip on the hammer he was holding and took a menacing step forward, his eyes glinting dangerously.

'Demetrius! What has happened to you? Is this man responsible?'

Ignoring Andreas, Mr Mourikis had moved to the other side of the car. Now he opened the door and bent to address someone inside.

'Leonidas! Get out before I drag you out!'

With obvious reluctance, another young man slowly got out of the car and shuffled round to face the people of the farm. Now they could see that he was even more beaten-up than Demetrius, with both eyes badly discoloured.

'This, to my shame, is my son Leonidas,' Paul Mourikis said, contemptuously indicating the youth with a disdainful finger. 'I apologise for not bringing these two sooner. I would have been here earlier if I could, but it took me some time to persuade the police to release them without charge.'

'The police!' Katerina's hand flew to her throat. 'Had they been arrested? What for?'

'They were causing a disturbance in a bar in Limassol last night. The police were called, and when they arrived, these two were on the floor apparently trying to kill each other. The police kept them in the cells overnight to cool them down. My son called me this morning and then I had to persuade the police that there was little point in taking two drunken students to court when they hadn't damaged anything except each other.'

Andreas took another step forward.

'I have seen your son before. He came here with Demetrius. Why were two friends fighting?'

Mr Mourikis's lips curled in disgust.

'Because your brother had discovered that Leonidas is a fool and a criminal.'

His son started to say something in protest and was silenced with a casual back-handed slap by his father which nearly knocked him off his feet. Everybody else waited to hear more.

'It took me some time to get the full truth from him. I think even he was ashamed. After he came here — after you had received him in your home as your guest — Leonidas began to think how he could make money out of you. I understand Demetrius had told him that it was proving hard to keep the farm going.'

'He decided that if the farmhouse were to be destroyed you would have to sell up, so he planned to burn the house down. Then, when you were desperate for money he would offer to buy you out. After that, he was going to come to me, tell me that he could get some good land for development at a very reasonable price.'

'His 'reasonable price' was going to be about twice what he had offered you. Then he was going to take my money, pay you what you had agreed, and pocket the rest of the money.'

He turned and surveyed the house.

'Fortunately he was as incompetent as an arsonist as he is at everything else. I understand that a shed was burned down and I can see some smoke stains, but the main building seems undamaged. Let me have a bill for the cost of replacing the shed and what any other repairs cost you and I will pay it.'

'There is no need for that,' Andreas said stiffly, and Mourikis shook his head violently.

'You do not understand. You will be doing me a kindness. I feel dishonoured by what my son has done. If I can pay, at least I will feel a little less ashamed.' He turned to Leonidas. 'As for my son, he is my only child and I have obviously been too lax with him, but now he is going to reform.'

'No more college and student life for him — tomorrow he will start work in my business, and I will see that he is made to work very hard indeed. Meanwhile, I leave your brother with you. Don't be hard on him. He was trying to avenge you. I would change him for my son any day.'

He turned to his car, gesturing abruptly at Leonidas who hastily climbed in the back seat. With one hand on the driver's door, Mourikis turned to Andreas.

'One more thing. I want to make it clear that I would not have bought your farm, however low the price. My son was too stupid to realise that it is too far from the sea, too out of the way to interest investors.'

He nodded abruptly at the small group, slid into the driving seat, started the big car and left as quickly as he had come, leaving them all staring after him. Then Andreas turned to Demetrius, who had been standing silently by, his head hanging low.

'What have you to add to that?'

Aunt Anne interrupted briskly.

'Andreas, the lad will tell us everything, but it is obvious that first of all he needs to have a shower and change his clothes. Then he can tell us his side of the story.'

Demetrius shot her a grateful look and, at a nod from his brother, hurried into the house.

* * *

All thought of leaving for the hotel was forgotten. They wanted to hear what Demetrius had to say. Katerina brought out coffee and wine, and they sat wondering at what Mourikis had told them until Demetrius rejoined them in clean jeans and a T-shirt. He subsided into the chair Andreas pushed towards him. Everybody was looking at him expectantly, but he said nothing until

Katrina had given him a cup of coffee and he had mumbled his thanks before draining it thirstily.

The suspense was proving too much for Andreas.

'Well?' he snapped impatiently.

Demetrius swallowed, looking at his brother from under his brows.

'When I went to see Katerina at the hotel yesterday she wasn't there, but these two (indicating Lorna and James) saw me and told me about the fire here. It was clear that they thought I was responsible.'

'Then I remembered a conversation I had had with Leonidas, when we were discussing landowners who were reluctant to sell. He said it was often their home they loved, not their land, and that if the home was gone they were usually willing to sell. I asked him how the home could be removed, and he laughed and said, 'Burn them out.' I also remembered how he had looked at our farm and started working out how many villas could be built on our fields.'

'So I went to Limassol, found him in a bar, and demanded to know if he had been responsible for the fire. He denied it, but I persisted because I didn't believe him, and in the end he said of course he had done it, and that if I had had any sense I would have burned the place down myself ages ago.' The boy's voice rose.

'I was so angry that I threw myself at him. We were rolling over and over on the floor, and then the police arrived and arrested us.' He shivered. 'A night in prison is not a pleasant experience. In the morning Leonadis's father came and got us out and made us tell him why we had been fighting.' His eyes widened. 'Do you know, he shook Leonidas by the scruff of the neck as if he were a puppy.' Now he sat back and looked unhappily round the little circle of intent faces. 'I'm sorry. I have been a fool, thinking only of myself. I was responsible for bringing Leonidas here. Can you forgive me?'

Katerina stretched her arm across the

table and took her young brother's hand in hers.

'Of course we can,' she said softly, and glared at Andreas until he nodded and echoed her statement.

'We can, yes, provided you show you have learned your lesson.'

'I have! I spent a long, uncomfortable night thinking about everything. I am going to leave college and work beside you on the farm . . .'

'Nonsense!' Katerina interrupted. 'You can help Andreas when he needs it, but you must have a career as well. The farm cannot support a family, that much is true.'

'Well, we will leave the three of you to discuss that,' Aunt Anne interjected. 'I think it's high time we were getting back to the hotel. Come along, you two.'

James shook his head.

'You go and wait in the jeep. I want a word with Demetrius first — in private.'

With his elder brother and sister looking after him anxiously, Demetrius was steered into the privacy of the house by James. Lorna followed them to find James confronting Demetrius, hands on hips.

'Arson wasn't the only crime committed that night,' he said crisply. 'We told you that the local church was robbed. Most of the silver was abandoned and we found it and returned it, but the lid of a chalice is still missing. Did you happen to find out anything about that?'

A faint smile glimmered on Demetrius's lips. He crossed to where he had hung up the jacket he had been wearing, put a hand into the pocket, pulled out a small object, and handed it to James. It was a silver domed lid, heavily chased.

'When Leonidas admitted — or rather, boasted — that he had tried to bum down the farm, he also told me that he had robbed the church. He said it deserved to be robbed for not taking better care of its valuables. Then he showed me the lid and said he was sorry he had lost the rest.'

'I grabbed the lid from him when we were fighting.' He sighed, staring down at the floor. 'He had been my friend before, so I did not tell his father. Mr Mourikis would have killed him outright if he had known he was guilty of such a crime.'

'Then let's keep the secret between the three of us,' said James. 'I'll return the lid. Now get back to Katerina and Andreas and tell them how good you are going to be in the future!'

As they set off in the jeep Aunt Anne was obviously longing to know what they had been discussing with Demetrius, but their evasive answers soon showed her that she would get no satisfaction and she subsided into a rather sulky silence.

She sat up alertly, however, when James braked outside the little church.

'What's the matter? Has something gone wrong with this awful vehicle?'

'Nothing's wrong,' James returned. 'Lorna and I just want to see to something. We won't be five minutes. You can stay here.'

★ ★ ★

Today when he pushed open the church door there was candlelight and the smell of incense and a priest in black robes stood near the altar.

He turned at the sound of their footsteps and when Lorna saw the grey beard and stern face she realised with a shock that the priest was the shirt-sleeved man with the shotgun that they had encountered in this very place the other night.

Now he waited in silent dignity for them to approach. Lorna and James halted in front of him and James held out his hand. The silver lid of the chalice gleamed softly on his palm. The priest took it from him and examined it, then turned and placed it carefully on the chalice. Then he turned back to them.

'I am grateful to you. Are you able to

tell me how you managed this?'

James shook his head.

'It would involve too many people. The thief will be punished for other crimes. I can assure you, however, that the person who actually gave it to me to return to you was not guilty of the theft, but has now repented of their other faults.'

The priest's white teeth gleamed in an unexpected smile.

'Perhaps I can guess something of the story. There is always gossip in a small village. I am glad to hear that the young man has realised what his faults were and I shall remember him in my prayers.'

As they returned to the jeep Lorna realised that James had taken her hand as they stood before the priest and was still holding it, though he released it to climb into the vehicle.

Then they saw that the priest was standing at the church door and they both waved goodbye. The priest waved back, smiling broadly, before re-entering the church, leaving the doors open, as was always the custom.

'I suppose it is too much to ask what on earth is going on this time,' Aunt Anne said icily.

'It is,' James said cheerfully as they drove off, and Lorna hastened to add, 'It's not our secret, Aunt Anne. All we can say is that all the silver has now been returned.'

In an attempt to cheer up her aunt, she added, 'At least now Mr Mourikis is willing to pay for the damage his son caused, the crisis is over. Andreas won't have to sell the farm.'

'You mean the crisis has been postponed. Nothing has really altered,' was her aunt's comment, and there was an ominous silence in the back seat for the rest of the way back to the Hotel Persepolis.

They were so late that it was a rush to wash and change in time for dinner before service ended and afterwards some friends of Aunt Anne insisted that she and Lorna joined them in the lounge where dancers were performing what were described as typical Cypriot dances.

Looking at the girls' skimpy costumes, Lorna found it difficult to believe this, and then scolded herself for thinking like a prissy middle-aged spinster.

Finally Aunt Anne decided that it was time for bed and led Lorna towards the lifts.

Lorna, who had been nervously expecting an interrogation all evening, was just inserting her key into her bedroom door while wishing Aunt Anne good-night and deciding that she had misjudged the extent of her aunt's curiosity, when a hand grasped her wrist firmly.

'Don't be in such a hurry to get away from me,' her aunt said silkily. 'Now, I know you don't want to tell me everything, but I'm not dim. You and James go to a church where the priest appears to be waiting for you, and then you come out smiling and holding hands. This is after you have spent days going everywhere together.'

'Don't tell me it was just because of the silver. Now I don't know what the two of you are planning, and I know I said you needed some romance in your life, but if you are investigating the possibility of a quick wedding in Cyprus I advise you to reconsider. Your family would be very hurt if you did anything like that. Your mother would be heartbroken. She's been planning your wedding since the day you were born.'

Lorna stared at her, and then broke into laughter.

'Aunt Anne, it was nothing like that!'

Her aunt's face fell.

'Oh! Are you quite sure?'

'Of course I am! You have jumped to the wrong conclusions! James and I have only known each other for a few days, and we certainly don't have any romantic feelings for each other. We are friends, that's all. We were just glad that we had been able to clear up that matter with the priest to do with the silver I told you about.'

Aunt Anne sighed. 'What a pity! As I've said before, a little romance would do you good, Lorna. Well, good night.'

She opened her own door and shut it firmly behind her, leaving a disconcerted Lorna fumbling with her own lock for some seconds. Her feelings were a mixture of amusement and surprise. Fancy Aunt Anne thinking that James was interested in her! Couldn't she see how he felt about Katerina?

10

The following morning was rather an anticlimax. James went off in the jeep to continue working at the farm, but Lorna stayed at the hotel because Katerina would be there on duty. In fact she managed a word with her at mid-morning, but there was only time for the girl to tell her that it had been decided that Demetrius would continue at college but was also going to do a lot more on the farm, before a coach-load of tourists arrived and claimed all her attention.

Aunt Anne did not seem to wish for her niece's company and Lorna saw her deep in conversation with Ben. At lunch she said she would be going out for a couple of hours.

'Are you going shopping? Shall I come with you?' Lorna enquired dutifully, but her aunt shook her head.

'I shall be perfectly all right on my own, thank you.'

Lorna spent the afternoon swimming and sunbathing. This time to herself should have been precious, but in fact she felt decidedly lonely and was quite pleased when she saw Aunt Anne coming in the front entrance. Her aunt was clutching a business-like file which seemed to be bursting with papers but showed no wish to tell her niece what she had been doing, and instead of joining her by the pool went up to her room and did not come down till dinner. Even then she was quiet and seemed preoccupied.

Lorna started looking around for James but there was no sign of him and Katerina, who was back on duty for a second shift, informed her that he had intended to spend the night at the farm, while she herself would be staying at the hotel, ready for the morning shift the following day.

'James seems to be a part of your family now,' Lorna said a little bitterly and Katerina laughed and nodded.

'Andreas loves Demetrius, in spite of his faults, but I think that if he could choose another brother it would definitely be James.'

Perhaps Andreas would think that James as a brother-in-law would be nearly as good. Well, in a few days she would be back in England, back at work, and she would never see Katerina or her brothers again, and would probably never find out whether James did indeed come back to the island and to Katerina.

How long was it now to the end of her holiday? She did some brief calculations and nearly fell off her chair. Only two more full days in Cyprus, and then she would be flying home! Where had the holiday gone?

Just then she saw Aunt Anne approaching her purposefully, closely followed by Ben.

'Lorna, you haven't planned anything for tomorrow, have you?'

Lorna shook her head.

'Good. Someone will be picking us up at nine o'clock to take us to Andreas' farm. He'll take Katerina as well.' Aunt Anne turned to Ben. 'Thank you for all your help and advice, Ben.'

'I was delighted to be of assistance,' the travel rep replied with a friendly smile. 'I just hope your plans work out. You must let me know.'

'If they do, I'll see you.'

Ben left them, summoned by another client, while Lorna looked questioningly at her aunt.

'What plans are these?'

'Oh, just some ideas I've had,' her aunt said teasingly. 'And what is the matter with you? You looked quite upset.'

Lorna leaned back and sighed.

'I've just realised that we only have two days left before we go home.'

'Then you have enjoyed your holiday?'

'Oh, yes!' She turned to her aunt. 'You know I wasn't expecting to enjoy it much, but in fact I have had a wonderful time. The island is beautiful, I've met some people I really like, I've had some exciting experiences . . . maybe I haven't had the romantic encounter you were hoping I would, but it has been my best holiday ever, and I am very glad you brought me!'

Aunt Anne was looking decidedly smug.

'I knew you would. And it isn't over yet. Wait till tomorrow.'

And that was all she would say.

Lorna was expecting a taxi or saloon car to pick them up the next morning, but at nine o'clock a battered, dusty, very basic four-wheel drive vehicle appeared. The man who got out and greeted Aunt Anne before turning to the two girls was tall and broad-shouldered, dressed in a khaki shirt and combat trousers which were both in need of a good ironing.

Aunt Anne introduced him.

'This is Mr Karamanlis. He is with a Cypriot organisation which promotes tourism in the country,' she announced with a smile and a flourish of her hand.

'Call me Nicholas,' the driver said. 'Miss Short, you can sit by me. You two girls, watch your step as you get into this contraption, and just move anything that is on the seats.'

'Anything' proved to be assorted tools and files of paper, as well as a couple of cameras.

The seats were hard and unyielding and Nicholas's casual style of driving, with one hand on the wheel and the other gesticulating as he pointed out items of interest, had Lorna wistfully recalling James's careful driving. They reached the farm with surprising speed, and Lorna and Katerina climbed gratefully down. When Andreas appeared, it seemed he was expecting Nicholas

'Miss Short telephoned me and told me that you were coming,' he said, shaking hands. 'She wasn't very clear what the purpose of your visit was.'

'I can explain properly now,' Aunt Anne interrupted, 'but first of all Nicholas needs to be shown the house

— all of it. Lorna and Katerina, you could have some coffee ready for us when we get back. We'll probably be about half an hour.'

Itching with curiosity though they were, the two girls had no choice but to do as they were told. Katerina was totally baffled.

'I know Cyprus wants more tourists but that seems to mean more hotels by the sea. What does he want to see here?'

At this point Maria appeared, wobbling along on a very old bicycle. She asked exactly the same question when the situation was explained to her, but they could do nothing but wait until the other three re-appeared a good hour later.

At least they seemed to be in a good humour, but insisted on having their coffee before they would explain. Lorna was beginning to believe that nobody on Cyprus could explain anything until coffee had been drunk.

'As it was Miss Short's idea, she will tell you all about it,' Andreas told them.

Aunt Anne was in no hurry to finish her coffee. Her niece suspected she was enjoying prolonging the wait and keeping them in suspense, but just as Lorna was on the point of losing her temper with her aunt, the lady sat up straight and looked around the little circle of faces, coughed importantly, and launched into her speech.

'Well, you all know how important tourism is to Cyprus, but not everybody has yet realised that there are different types of tourists. Most will want the traditional sun, sea and sand, while others come to see the remains of ancient civilisations, but there is a growing number who want to see another aspect of the island — its landscapes, flowers and animals such as the moufflons, the wild sheep with the big horns.'

'The last thing these people want is to destroy the environment and landscape and they don't like big hotels. Many of them walk or cycle from place to place, and they like to stay one or two nights at a farm or in a private house.'

Lorna looked round and saw that the others had realised where this was leading.

'Andreas's farm would be ideal for these tourists. The Akamas peninsula offers everything they want to see. There is unspoiled country for the walkers and plants such as orchids and cyclamens for the nature-lovers. There are four bedrooms in the main part of the house that could be used by tourists and Andreas could offer them bed and breakfast and feed them in the evening. That would be all they would need, so a couple could run the business as well as the farm.'

Lorna saw Andreas glance swiftly at Maria, who was leaning forward, her eyes glowing, but Aunt Anne's voice had changed, growing sterner.

'Unfortunately the rooms cannot be rented as they are. They need decorating and furnishing and guests who are sweaty and dusty after a day exploring

Cyprus will want en suite bathrooms. This will need considerable investment, and it is no secret that Andreas and Katerina do not have the money required.'

Maria looked as if she was about to burst into tears as her hopes were dashed, but Aunt Anne had not finished.

'However, there is a solution. I want to buy the spare wing as a holiday home in Cyprus. The price would enable Andreas to carry out the necessary work to the bedrooms, and to start to refurbish the spare wing for me, as well as leaving enough cash to satisfy Agnes. Katerina, Andreas is willing to sell me the wing. What about you?'

Katerina sat for perhaps thirty seconds, gazing at her hands clasped in her lap. Then she nodded.

'I know there is a demand for such accommodation, for many guests at the hotel have told me how they would like to explore Cyprus at their own pace instead of having to get back to the hotel each night. As for selling part of the house, I think we will make good neighbours. So, yes, I agree.'

Aunt Anne was beaming.

'Thank you, Katerina. I understand from Andreas that Demetrius will agree to whatever he wants, and I am sure that even your sister Agnes will be pleased.'

'We also thought that when I am not using my part of the house it would make a good base for a family of holidaymakers, and I would, of course, pay Andreas a fee for looking after it.' She looked round. 'There are a few details still to be decided, but I spent a lot of time with lawyers yesterday, and there are no big obstacles to the plan. Any comments?'

Katerina and Andreas both wanted to clarify certain points, while Maria listened happily. James caught Lorna's eye and signalled that they should leave the rest to it. Side by side they strolled away towards the fields.

'This should solve a lot of problems,'

was James's first remark and Lorna agreed.

'I don't think this is an impulse that Aunt Anne will regret later. She has come to Cyprus many times and I know she loves the island. A place of her own with neighbours she likes will suit her very well, and Paphos is not far away if she wants the bright lights.'

'How do you feel? After all, you seem to be your aunt's favourite niece. Is this your inheritance she is spending?'

Lorna laughed.

'The money is hers to spend on what she wants and, anyway, I think my aunt is good for another twenty years at least.' She sighed. 'At least Maria will finally be able to start planning her wedding to Andreas. Do you think we will be invited?'

'I should hope so! And they will get one of my olive wood sculptures as a wedding present.'

Lorna stole a look at him as they strolled on. He wasn't conventionally good-looking, but he had a pleasant face, with a firm mouth and laughter lines already forming at the corners of his eyes. His relaxed air made people overlook the well-muscled body which moved with casual grace. She would miss him very much, and hoped that Katerina would appreciate him.

'Shall we go back?' he enquired, and they got back to the farm to find everyone toasting a satisfactory outcome to the negotiations.

Aunt Anne and Andreas, together with Katerina, had made an appointment to meet the lawyer who had been consulted and would arrange for contracts to be drawn up, so after a simple lunch they all set off for Paphos. Lorna and Katerina politely declined Nicholas's offer of a lift and went with Andreas in his van.

★   ★   ★

Back at the Hotel Persepolis with a free afternoon ahead, Lorna and James settled companionably side by side in deck chairs under trees which shaded them from the heat of the sun. They both read, or pretended to read, for both of them had a lot to think about.

'We can't keep calling Aunt Anne's holiday home 'the spare wing',' Lorna said suddenly. 'Can you think of a name?'

'How about calling it the 'Aunt's House'? It's the kind of name houses acquire,' James responded idly. He thought for a while longer and then said suddenly, 'It is the perfect place for a honeymoon.'

Lorna stared at him.

'You don't want to spend your honeymoon next door to your brother!'

James looked at her in confusion.

'Who on earth are you talking about, Lorna? He furrowed his brow.'

'Katerina!'

He laughed and shook his head.

'No chance! Katerina wants to go to Spain for her honeymoon.'

So the relationship had got far enough to start discussing honeymoons!

James suddenly leaned across and seized her arm.

'And here comes Katerina! Things must have gone very smoothly at the lawyer's office.'

Katerina, still wearing the jeans and T-shirt that she wore on the farm, had come onto the terrace and was obviously looking for somebody. Lorna was about to wave at her to signal their whereabouts when Alex, the under-manager, also appeared on the terrace. Was he going to rebuke the girl for her informal dress? But when Alex said something to Katerina she laughed and seemed to be telling him something. It must have been good news, for he too began to smile and then to laugh, and then, while the holidaymakers watched in amazement, he seized Katerina round the waist, lifted her up and set her down, and then kissed her soundly. Then the two of them disappeared inside the hotel.

Lorna gaped and then turned to look at James, expecting him to be appalled at the sight of the girl he loved kissing another man. But he was smiling broadly.

'James! What does he think he's doing?'

James settled back comfortably.

'I expect she is telling him what is going to happen at the farm.'

'But why should that make him kiss her?'

James gave her a look of disbelief.

'But didn't you know . . . ? Hadn't you guessed..? Katerina and Alex love each other, and they will be able to think of marrying now that her wages aren't needed to help with the farm. Andreas told me, but you've spent so much time with his sister that I thought she might have told you.'

Lorna thought back.

'Of course, Alex did say once that he had been out to the farm. I should have guessed — but I thought it was someone else.'

'Oh, Katerina is a fine girl, in fact I am very fond of her myself, but apparently there has never been anyone else but Alex.'

Mercifully he didn't ask who she had been thinking of and she sat quietly trying to readjust her thoughts.

'Then when you said my aunt's house would be the perfect place for a honeymoon, who were you thinking of?'

'I was thinking of us,' James said abstractedly, and then sat up abruptly, eyes wide. 'I didn't mean to say that — not yet!'

But Lorna was staring at him.

'You have been thinking of us getting married?' she said slowly, her heart racing, and James nodded reluctantly in his reply.

'These last few days, with the end of the holiday approaching, I realised that I couldn't say goodbye to you because I had fallen in love with you, Lorna. But I was going to take things slowly. Now I've been fool enough to blurt out how I feel I suppose you are going to tell me that you are not interested, that I haven't a chance.'

She shook her head.

'No, but then I thought you were interested in someone else.'

He gazed at her, puzzled.

'Who else could there be?'

'No one really,' she said hurriedly. 'I just got the impression that you did care for someone.'

'You,' James said firmly.

'Why?'

'We suit each other.'

'An accountant with the Inland Revenue and an artist?'

'Of course. We complement each other.'

A smile slowly curled her lips.

'I suppose we do.'

'Does that mean I have a chance? That you will consider marrying me?'

She snuggled down into her chair.

'I'll think about it. I warn you, it may take some time.'

At this moment they heard a voice behind them.

'There you are! I need a sit-down and a drink.'

It was her aunt. Lorna sat up and

contemplated her.

'Aunt Anne.'

'Yes, Lorna?'

'Will you please go away and find your drink and your chair somewhere else? James and I have a lot to discuss.'

Her aunt blinked and then studied her carefully.

'And will you tell me all about it afterwards?'

'I promise.'

Without another word Aunt Anne strode off towards the hotel. James and Lorna watched her go in a state of shock. Then James smiled triumphantly at Lorna.

'You will have to marry me now. That will be the only acceptable excuse for your behaviour.'

Lorna smiled back at him, with amusement ahd happiness sparkling in her eyes. 'I think you are right.'

Back in the hotel near the bar, Aunt Anne met Ben, the travel rep. He lifted an enquiring eyebrow at the sight of her.

'Did everything go smoothly?'

Aunt Anne nodded.

'The contracts will soon be ready and by next summer the farm should be ready to receive tourists.'

'And the other matter?'

'Look over there!'

She pointed out into the gardens, where James and Lorna were holding hands and laughing happily.

'Well done, my dear!' said Ben.

She patted her hair.

'Yes, I think I have done rather well. Mission accomplished.'

We do hope that you have enjoyed reading this large print book.

Did you know that all of our titles are available for purchase?

We publish a wide range of high quality large print books including:
Romances, Mysteries, Classics
General Fiction
Non Fiction and Westerns

Special interest titles available in large print are:
The Little Oxford Dictionary
Music Book, Song Book
Hymn Book, Service Book

Also available from us courtesy of Oxford University Press:
Young Readers' Dictionary
(large print edition)
Young Readers' Thesaurus
(large print edition)

For further information or a free brochure, please contact us at:
Ulverscroft Large Print Books Ltd.,
The Green, Bradgate Road, Anstey,
Leicester, LE7 7FU, England.
Tel: (00 44) **0116 236 4325**
Fax: (00 44) **0116 234 0205**

A BRIDE FOR
LORD MOUNTJOY

Karen Abbott

Georgiana's unchaperoned childhood ends when her father discovers her returning from a midnight jaunt with her brother and his friends. Squire Hailsham sends Georgiana to the Highpark Academy for Young Ladies in Brighton. There she enters High Society, where she attends elegant balls and meets dashing heroes. At the onset of a family tragedy, the eligible Lord Mountjoy crosses her path — but is he all that he seems? Does Georgiana risk breaking her heart when she discovers the truth?

VERA'S VICTORY

Anne Holman

World War II: As part of the war effort, Vera Carter has been instructed to adapt her Cordon Bleu cooking skills to running a British Restaurant in Norfolk. This is not her only worry — the staff she's been given are all untrained, and don't always get along with each other. And Geoffrey Parkington, the man in charge, seems to have very little sense of humour. But Vera soon discovers there is more to Geoffrey Parkington than she first thought . . .

FAMILY LIFE IN THE GLEN

Joan Christie

1903: Katy and Sandy Fraser's brood are fast growing up. The elder children are starting lives and families of their own, whilst the younger ones, though still at home, are starting to take their first tentative steps out into the wider world. But despite the joys it brings, family life can also be hard, and Catriona, their oldest daughter, will need everyone's support to come through tragedy and find happiness again . . .

MOLLY'S SECRET

Valerie Holmes

When Molly helps a man to escape from an old mill where two Ebton villagers have left him trussed up, she unwittingly changes her own destiny, her family's and that of the village. Her secret, if discovered, would have her ostracised. The opportunity to leave her simple life behind comes when the handsome Lieutenant James Deadman professes his love for her, asking her to be is wife. However, his cousin, Dr Russell Deadman, seems determined to foil their match . . .

FOLLOW YOUR HEART

Catriona McCuaig

When Ruby Byrne and her children emigrate to Canada in 1920, love is the last thing she expects to find. But when widower Robert Kerr proposes, she is happy to accept. Cait is pleased for her mother, yet she can't help thinking about her former fiancé, Trevor Thomas, back in Cardiff. Robert's son, Martin, is determined to win Cait as his bride, but is it fair to marry him when Trevor is still in her heart?

THE GIFT OF LOVE

Jean M. Long

When young Toby's mother, Jane, dies, his Aunt Shona and her family rally round to look after him. Shona helps to run Jane's Florist, selling the roses from her father's nursery. Then another cloud looms on the horizon. Mrs Tynedale, the elderly owner of the land on which the nursery stands, is considering selling up. Her grandson, Mallory, has come to help her make the right decision. Shona soon learns that mixing business with pleasure can lead to heartbreak.